"May I [...] Highness?" Chase asked

He led her down from the raised dais. Molly's right hand fit small and cool in his. Up close her emeralds were exquisite and worth a fortune. Surprisingly, he noted they were the same color as her eyes. Beautiful, mesmerizing eyes.

The princess tilted her chin up to look at him, an amused glimmer in those eyes. "You're drooling, Mr. Sanquist."

"Forgive me, Highness. I've never danced with a princess before."

"You mean, with such expensive jewels."

"Are you calling me a liar?"

"No, Mr. Sanquist. I'm calling you a thief."

So the princess did know who he was. He pulled her closer and smiled seductively. "I'd rather you call me Chase."

The stroke of his fingertips on the small of her back made Molly shiver. It was nothing personal, merely an involuntary reaction, her body adjusting from the drafty foyer to the overwarm ballroom.

"You needn't be so obvious," she replied. "I have every intention of inviting you to my bedroom." That surprised him, and she smiled in pleasure as she leaned closer, whispering, "For the jewels, of course."

Talented and versatile **Lynn Michaels,** who also writes as Paula Christopher, is an award-winning, bestselling author who specializes in unusual but always intriguing stories. Known for her humor and fast pacing, she often jokes that if it weren't for the weird stuff, she'd have nothing to write about. Luckily, she finds weird stuff at every turn.

Lynn, her husband and their two boys make their home in Missouri. She would love to hear from her readers. Write to her c/o Harlequin Temptation, 225 Duncan Mill Road, Don Mills, Ontario, Canada M3B 3K9.

Books by Lynn Michaels

HARLEQUIN TEMPTATION
304—REMEMBRANCE
405—THE PATRIOT
449—SECOND SIGHT
481—AFTERSHOCK

MOLLY AND THE PHANTOM
LYNN MICHAELS

All characters in this book have no existence outside the imagination of the author and have no relation whatsoever to anyone bearing the same name or names. They are not even distantly inspired by any individual known or unknown to the author, and all the incidents are pure invention.

Harlequin Books

**TORONTO • NEW YORK • LONDON
AMSTERDAM • PARIS • SYDNEY • HAMBURG
STOCKHOLM • ATHENS • TOKYO • MILAN
MADRID • WARSAW • BUDAPEST • AUCKLAND**

For Nancy,
the "woo-woo" queen

ISBN 0-373-25611-6

MOLLY AND THE PHANTOM

Copyright © 1994 by Lynne Smith.

Printed in U.S.A.

Prologue

"The Phantom of St. Cristobel"
from Fabulous Jewels and Their Fabulous Myths
By Sir Ivor Smythe-Byington

*It is not the spectacular size, 532 carats, marvelous color and
exceptional clarity of the Phantom of St. Cristobel that most
attracts attention. Rather, like King Tut's tomb, it is the
curse.*

*Most likely mined in the same region of India that pro-
duced the Hope Diamond, another rare and supposedly
cursed sapphire blue diamond, the Phantom is the largest
and one of the oldest cut stones known to man. Referred to
in antiquity as the Phantom of Thar and the Phantom of
Rub al Khali, it is believed to be the "Great Eye of Allah"
mentioned in the writings of the sixth-century Arab scholar
Hammad.*

*Legend claims that the stone was captured by Sir Ossric
of Glyco from Sultan Saddiq el Shehabi during the Crusades in Palestine in 1192. It also claims that before his be-
heading by the Scottish knight, Sultan Shehabi cursed Sir
Ossric and all his male issue, calling upon Allah to grant the
Laird of Glyco and all his heirs who touched the Phantom
everything their hearts desire.*

*The Sanquists of Glyco prospered until Laird Ian, fifth
earl of Glyco and a complete wastrel, discovered the hard*

way what Sultan Shehabi knew, that a prudent man was careful what he wished for. On his way to Edinburgh in 1730, where he planned to gamble himself out of the dissolute life-style he believed was due to the stone, Laird Ian wished fervently never to lay eyes on the Phantom again.

His wish was apparently granted, for when he passed out drunk at the gaming tables, the stone was stolen along with his purse. Although no record of this theft can be found, it is known that Laird Ian Sanquist, deeply in debt and unable to borrow further on his heavily mortgaged estates, took the gentleman's way out and shot himself.

Several Highland ballads written over the next decade are said to be based on the exploits of Laird Ian's son, Anthony Sanquist, who was forced to become a highwayman to rescue the family from ruin. The most famous of these ballads, sung to this day in local pubs, is "The Midnight Rogue."

No further record of the Phantom can be found until 1752, when the stone surfaced in the European principality of St. Cristobel, where it was mounted in the royal scepter and declared by the Bishop of San Blanco to be a sign from God of the Savard Dynasty's divine right to rule. Laird Ian of Glyco's grandson, Chastain Sanquist, was beheaded in St. Cristobel in 1786 for trying to steal the jewel from Crown Prince Sandor I. Upon his death, the title Earl of Glyco passed to an English branch of the Sanquist family.

Long a time-honored tradition in the Highlands, robbery continued to be the mainstay of the Lairds of Glyco through the ascension of George V to the British throne. Many allegations of thievery against them can be found in parish records, though none was ever proven. Ironically, and all great legends lean heavily upon irony, most were charges of jewel theft.

It is known that the Lairds of Glyco did for a time possess a "raree jewel" said to be nearly the same color as "the bonny wee heather in bloome." Neither such charming notations in histories of the time, nor Laird Ian's bloodstained suicide note, have served as sufficient proof of ownership in the many courts of law in which the Sanquist family has sought over the years to reclaim the stone.

Neither historians, gemologists or anyone with both feet planted firmly in the twentieth century can give credence to the notion that the Phantom, or indeed any stone, is cursed. Archaeologists tell us that such stories are created out of a sense of awe, as a means of accounting for events that appear to be beyond human control. They can do much to increase the value of a stone with little intrinsic worth, though this is certainly not the case with the Phantom, which remains the most valuable of all privately owned diamonds in the world.

A final tragic footnote was added to the history of the stone in 1973, when Phillip Sanquist, cousin of Ian Sanquist, then Fifteenth Earl of Glyco, and his American wife, Linda, were killed in an avalanche in the French Alps while on a skiing holiday. The accident occurred near enough to the border of St. Cristobel to give rise to rumors of another failed attempt to reclaim the stone.

Cursed or not, the Phantom remains in St. Cristobel, where it is the centerpiece of the fabulous Crown jewels, which are described in a later chapter.

1

SHE WAS BORN a princess but you'd never know it to look at her. Any more than you'd know just by looking at Chase Sanquist that he ranked third on Interpol's most-wanted list. He no more looked a thief than Her Serene Highness Marie-Marguerite Christiana Alistrina Helene Savard looked born to rule the tiny principality of St. Cristobel.

In a Chicago Bears baseball cap, jeans and a red sweatshirt over a white turtleneck, she looked born to marry an accountant and attend PTA meetings. Her knee-high jodhpur boots gave her outfit just a dash of Continental chic, enough to make the Princess Molly—so called because Her Highness refused to answer to anything but the nickname given her by her American mother—look all the rage in Europe.

Trailing a discreet half block or so behind the princess along Parabello Street, the Rodeo Drive of San Blanco, the capital of St. Cristobel, Chase looked a typical wealthy tourist in Gucci loafers and gray pleated trousers. The sleeves of his striped silk-blend shirt were rolled to the elbows, a Ralph Lauren sweater knotted around his shoulders.

When the princess slid her dark glasses down her upturned nose to take a closer look at something in a shop window, Chase swung away from her, lifted the Nikon looped around his neck and squinted into the lens. The viewfinder showed him a panoramic sweep of Alpine peaks ringing the far borders of St. Cristobel in a majestic, blue-gray haze.

The light meter he raised showed him a tiny red blip on a grid less than half the size of the screen on a pocket video game. Chase smiled. The bug he'd dropped into the suit-coat pocket of the princess' bodyguard four blocks ago was working perfectly.

Her Highness shrugged and moved on. Chase went with her, the bodyguard following a few yards behind. Planting the bug had been child's play, the first of many skills Chase had learned from his uncle Cosmo.

"Once you've mastered the art of putting things into pockets," he'd told his orphaned twelve-year-old American nephew some twenty years earlier, "we'll move on to taking things out."

Which nimble-fingered Chase had done within six months. By his thirteenth birthday he'd lifted enough to enable Cosmo to move them west from London's dreary East End into a charming flat much closer to the hotels and tourist haunts that were their stock-in-trade.

"You're a natural, my boy," his uncle had told him proudly. "A throwback to Chastain Sanquist himself."

Chase had been in St. Cristobel for a week, for the last three days following the princess on her afternoon shopping forays. By the number of packages she carried, emblazoned with names like Gucci, Dior and Chanel, you'd never guess St. Cristobel was in the throes of its worst economic depression since the end of World War II.

If you lived in a palace filled with more treasures than the Louvre, money was obviously not a problem. But if your birthright was a five-hundred-year-old castle in Scotland, a towering pile of rock with more drafts than a last-place team in the National Football League, you could never earn—or steal—enough to support it.

Filthy rich as the princess was, losing the Phantom would hardly dent her personal fortune. Chase was always careful never to steal more than a mark could afford to lose. Unlike some people's ancestors, who'd blithely ripped his off and cast them into ruin.

The two plainclothes guards who'd followed the princess from the palace were still trailing her on the other side of the street. Chase hadn't bothered to bug them. There was no need; wherever the princess and her bodyguard went, so did they. And so would Chase, until the opportunity to make her acquaintance presented itself.

From there, he planned to charm his way into her bedroom in the south wing of the palace. The Phantom spent its nights there in a room-size safe behind a shimmering high-tech security grid similar to the one that protected it from nine to four-thirty Monday through Friday while it sat on display with the rest of the St. Cristobel Crown jewels. The treasury made a pile off the tourists who plunked down five francs to tour the palace and behold the fabled Phantom, surrounded by lesser diamonds, rubies, emeralds and a king's ransom worth of gold and platinum in the royal scepter.

Disabling or fooling the grid wouldn't be difficult, but it would take time. More than Chase wanted to spend dodging palace guards and playing password with the computer-controlled security system. He'd decided on the plane from Edinburgh that it would be a hell of a lot easier if the princess simply invited him to see her etchings.

He had absolutely no doubt that she would. He might never make the "sexiest man alive" cover of *People* magazine, but he'd wooed his way into more than one boudoir. Her figure was a bit too willowy for his taste, her features too elfin, but at least she wasn't plug-ugly like most of the Savard women. Which was, Chase was sure, the reason no

Sanquist male had ever even remotely considered matrimony as a means of recovering the Phantom.

On the corner of Parabello and *rue de* Savard, the princess stopped and waited for the gendarme directing traffic on the center island to halt the cars zipping through the intersection at Formula One speeds. Chase stopped behind her, close enough to note the gold highlights in the thick brown ponytail stuck through the back of her cap. It was time, he decided, to pick up the pace. Her twenty-fifth birthday ball, the perfect setting for dancing her upstairs into bed, was tomorrow night.

He lifted the Nikon and looked into the lens. In the tiny mirror beside it, he saw the bodyguard, a dark-haired behemoth with a handlebar mustache, come to a halt in the crowd of pedestrians behind him. Next to him stood a woman in a beige mink jacket, a vivid pink tunic and leggings tucked into suede ankle boots. Her blond hair was swept under an electric-pink ball cap with silver stars studded on the brim. Her arms were draped with shopping bags, her features obscured by a huge pair of dark glasses.

She'd do nicely, Chase decided, watching the princess adjust her shoulder bag as he wound the film advance on the Nikon and wondered how she'd react if she knew they were distant cousins. Would she whip out his photo during an interview with a *Paris Match* reporter as she had the dog-eared tintype of her great-grandfather on her mother's side, hung as a horse thief in Arizona in 1876?

Clever piece of work, that. Her then beau, son of a German industrialist with semi-royal connections, hand-picked for her by her uncle Karroll, Grand Duke and Regent, had whisked himself off the ski slopes of St. Cristobel quicker than you can say giant slalom.

With baton held high in one white-gloved hand the gendarme stopped traffic. With the other he signaled the pe-

destrians. The princess stepped off the curb. Chase
followed, brushing close enough to the woman in mink to
get a noseful of Joy and hook a finger through the nylon
cord handles of the shopping bags looped over her arm.

They spilled at her feet as he moved past her, tumbling
smaller bags and boxes into the street and the gutter. She
tripped over a couple with a cry of dismay and bent to pick
them up. The bodyguard stopped to help her, just like Chase
figured he would. Glancing over his shoulder, Chase kept
walking. So did the princess.

The bodyguard snatched up the last package and pulled
the woman back on the curb. A second before the baton fell,
a heartbeat before Chase quickened his pace and made the
crossing—just barely—with a red Fiat convertible nearly
clipping his heels.

The driver gave him a sharp, angry toot of his horn, the
gendarme a shrill blast of his whistle. Chase spun around
with a sheepish who-me lift of his shoulders. The gendarme stood pointing at him, the bodyguard glaring. Chase
raised the Nikon, took a quick snap of the two of them, then
ducked after the princess.

His blood was singing, his pulse thudding. Nothing like
a close brush to get the old adrenaline pumping. He'd been
playing chicken with cars at crosswalks since he was four-
teen, and had yet to lose. It was the one thing, the only thing
he did that had ever come close to giving Cosmo heart fail-
ure. Until the day Chase announced he was going after the
Phantom.

The princess was about ten yards ahead of him now and
nearing her destination, an open-air café near the end of
Parabello Street where it tumbled down a long, cobbled hill
to the sea and the wharfs and marinas built around the
mouth of the bay. Invariably she stopped here to drink
cappuccino and bask in the early spring sunshine. Her

bodyguard usually gave her about half an hour before summoning the Rolls limo that would chauffeur her to the palace.

Chase quickened his steps as she veered off the sidewalk toward the entrance, fumbling for something in her shoulder bag as she pushed through the swinging, waist-high iron gate. One of the packages tucked inside, a gold foil sack, snagged on a black filigree and fell onto the sidewalk. Chase picked it up and checked his light meter one last time. Her bodyguard was a good twenty yards behind.

Smiling, he followed the princess into the café.

2

THE FIRST TIER of the terraced outdoor café was reserved for Her Serene Highness. The maître d' met her with a bow and led her through an artful maze of glass-topped tables protected from the gulls wheeling overhead by umbrellas striped in green and black, the national colors of St. Cristobel.

The maître d' bowed again as he lifted a green velvet rope, and the princess stepped past him with a nod. She dumped her packages in a black canvas chair and sat down in a green one with her face to the water and her back to the sun.

Chase gave her a minute to get settled and give her order to the waiter who came bowing to her side. When she leaned back, crossed her legs at the knee and bent her elbows on the arms of her chair, he wove his way toward her around orange trees budding in white-painted tubs. He checked the maître d', saw that he was busy seating a group of tourists, and stepped over the rope.

"Your Highness." He stopped in front of her and bowed as he offered her the gold bag. "You dropped this."

"Thank you." She smiled as she reached across the table to take it from him. She didn't look surprised, which was interesting. "This is my birthday gift to my uncle. How embarrasing it would be not to have one to give him at my birthday party tomorrow evening."

Her English was American with no discernible accent. She was fluent in French, Italian, German and Spanish, as well. So was Chase, but he stuck to English and the high-toned Brit inflections he'd picked up from Cosmo and his cousin Tony.

"The giving of gifts to others on your birthday is one of St. Cristobel's most charming customs," he said, straightening to find himself eye to eye with the bodyguard looming behind her left shoulder.

He was big as a boxcar, but obviously could move when he had to. Up close, he looked familiar. It took Chase a minute, but he finally recognized Danny "Driller" Diello, a former Chicago Bears All-Pro defensive end.

Now *this* was interesting. Driller Diello had put more running backs in casts than an orthopedic surgeon.

"If that gift is meant for your uncle you might want to be more careful with it," Chase said to the princess. "I didn't hear it ticking, but somebody else might."

She laughed, tucked the foil sack among the others, then leaned back in her chair and regarded him curiously. Her almond-shaped eyes were sea green tinged with amber, large and slightly upturned at the corners, her nose a little too short and pert to balance them against her very full mouth. He wouldn't have any trouble at all, Chase thought, rising to the occasion—so to speak—tomorrow night.

"How do you know my uncle? Are you a reporter?" She let her gaze drop to the Nikon and the light meter around his neck. "Or a photographer perhaps?"

"No, Your Highness. Merely a wealthy ne'er-do-well."

She laughed, her gold-threaded brown ponytail fluttering over one shoulder in a snatch of salty breeze. Obviously, she thought he was kidding. "And what reward do you expect for returning my package?"

She was quick. And direct. Chase liked that in a mark.

"Perhaps a dance tomorrow evening at your birthday ball?"

"I'm sorry. I'd love to invite you, but the guest list is strictly controlled by my uncle and my advisers."

"I have an invitation, Your Highness. My cousin the Earl of Glyco was unable to attend. I've come in his stead."

It wasn't a lie. He'd pinched the invitation off Tony's desk at Glyco. His cousin wouldn't miss it. Knowing Tony, he probably hadn't even known it was there.

"Indeed." The princess tipped her head to one side. "And your name is?"

"Sanquist, Your Highness. Chase Sanquist."

She knew the name. He saw it in her eyes, in the quick shift from amused glimmer to wary gleam. This was *very interesting.* Possibly even dangerous. Chase felt his pulse quicken. Danger was even better than sex. Well, almost.

"Tell me, Mr. Sanquist." The princess lifted her chin and regarded him coolly. "Have you come to St. Cristobel to dance with me or to steal my diamond?"

"Which diamond is that, Your Highness? You have so many—so I'm told," Chase added with a smile.

"I refer to Le Fantôme, Mr. Sanquist," she replied, calling the stone by its French name. "The diamond your forbearer lost some three hundred years ago. The diamond your family keeps trying to steal from mine."

"The Phantom wasn't lost, Your Highness. It was stolen."

"So you say. So your family has repeatedly said, in every court in every country that would hear your claim. Eight times your petition has been denied, last by the World Court in 1987. It seems you cannot produce sufficient evidence of ownership."

"Neither can you, Your Highness, since none exists."

The half smile lifting one corner of her mouth didn't change, but her eyes went from cool, sea-foam green to icy, angry amber. Diello took a step forward, but the princess raised a hand, and he stopped.

"Are you calling me a thief, Mr. Sanquist?"

"No, Your Highness. I'm calling Crown Prince Sandor the First a thief."

She laughed, her amusement warming her smile but not her eyes. The old stories said Sandor I himself had wielded the sword that killed Chastain Sanquist. Gazing steadily at his six times great-granddaughter, Chase believed it.

"I'm told it takes a thief to recognize a thief, Mr. Sanquist."

"I wouldn't know, Your Highness."

"But I believe we're both acquainted with someone who does." She gave him a regal, cat-in-the-cream smile. "Chief Inspector John Francis of Scotland Yard."

"Retired," Chase corrected her. "Yes, I've met Inspector Francis. He's an excellent choice to supervise security for your coronation next week."

Someone else might've missed the flicker in her smile, but not Chase. He knew as much about faces and body language as he did about gems. Especially diamonds, particularly the Phantom. He'd trumped her trump, and Her Serene Highness didn't like it.

"Inspector Francis said if I saw you I should lock you in the dungeons and throw away the key."

"I've heard about your dungeons. Crown Prince Caspar used them last during World War II. A hundred and fifty Nazi collaborators went in and never came out."

"He was my grandfather." The princess smiled. "I'm told I favor him."

She no more meant physically than Chase meant to leave St. Cristobel without the Phantom. It was a warning—and a challenge. Chase had never been able to pass up a good one.

"I disagree, Your Highness. You favor your mother. I look forward to seeing her again tomorrow evening."

Her right eyebrow arched dubiously. "*You* know my mother?"

"Not in the biblical sense, more's the pity," Natalie Vincennes Savard said, sweeping around Diello and dumping her shopping bags in the chair next to her daughter. She tugged off her pink ball cap, the one with the star-shaped studs on the brim, shook her fluffy blond hair around her shoulders, tucked her dark glasses in the pocket of her mink and smiled as she offered her hand. "Hello, Chase. How are you?"

"Natalie." He grinned, both surprised and delighted. "Weren't you a redhead at Wimbledon?"

"So was everyone else. That's why I'm a blonde. Doing Tony's duty again, are you?"

Chase released her hand, noting from the corner of his eye that the princess was doing her best not to look flabbergasted. She was attempting disinterest, despite the little flickering up and down glances she gave him.

"It keeps me out of trouble."

"That'll be the day. Are you coming tomorrow night?"

"I have an invitation."

"Molly, you must dance with Chase." Natalie linked her arm through his and turned to face her daughter. "He is the true mambo king."

"We were just discussing that, Mother."

"Were you? How marvelous." Natalie gave Chase an arch look. "But the mambo is mine."

"Always." Chase brought her hand to his lips, then nodded to her daughter. "Your Highness. I look forward to tomorrow evening."

"So do I, Mr. Sanquist. I'll save you a dance on my card." The princess inclined her chin, her eyes mostly green and glittering. "But not the mambo. Good day."

Chase bowed away from the table as Diello stepped forward to intercept the waiter. With his attention on the transfer of three white cups heaped with steaming frothed milk from the tray to the table, it was easy for Chase to brush close enough to retrieve the bug from his suit-coat pocket.

Slipping it into his own, he smiled and headed for the exit. He'd accomplished his first objective, meeting and impressing the princess.

Now it was time he met the Phantom.

3

"DOESN'T LOOK MUCH like a jewel thief, does he?" Molly asked, turning sideways in her chair to watch Chase Sanquist make his unhurried way out of the café.

"Who said he's a jewel thief?" Natalie demanded sharply.

"Inspector Francis," Molly replied, wondering how long it would take Chase Sanquist's ski-slope tan to fade in a dungeon.

"He's as bad as your uncle Karroll." Natalie slid out of her mink, draped it over a chair and sat down. "Neither one of them trusts their own shadow."

"Looks like what he says he is to me." Danny sat across from Molly, the canvas creaking under his nearly two hundred and fifty pounds of muscle. "A rich do-nothin'."

"Looks are deceiving," Molly said thoughtfully. "The same could be said about me."

Diello snorted and raised his cup. "Not by anybody who knows you."

"That's my point." Molly gave Chase a last, wistful once-over and turned around. "Nice tush, though."

Diello banged his cup down, a white froth on his mustache. "Forget about his tush."

"Down, Danny." Natalie laughed. "She's only going to dance with him."

More's the pity, Molly thought. She liked Chase Sanquist. Not for his blond, blue-eyed looks, though if he wasn't the handsomest man she'd ever seen he was definitely among them. She liked him because he'd had guts enough to approach her. Few men did, jewel thief or not. Those who weren't put off by the fact that she was a princess and above their touch were discouraged by Danny's glowering size.

Chase Sanquist hadn't been. He'd looked Danny straight in the eye. He'd recognized him, too. She'd bet her crown on it, which cast his upper-class British accent in doubt. What most Englishmen knew about American football wouldn't fill the eye of a needle.

"How long have you known him?" Molly folded her arms on the table and looked at her mother. "Where did you meet him?"

Natalie took a sip of her cappuccino and frowned. "You sound like Inspector Francis, Molly. Or your uncle Karroll."

"I *am* a princess, Mother. Protecting the Phantom is my number-one priority. This would not be a good time for it to turn up missing."

"'Specially since you plan to auction it at Sothebys next spring," Danny said, lifting his cup to his mouth again.

Molly could have choked him, but didn't have to. The mouthful of cappuccino he swallowed before he realized what he'd said took care of it for her. Nicely.

"That's the last time I tell you a state secret," she said, tossing him a green linen napkin.

"Sorry, kiddo," he managed to gasp, then buried his face in the napkin and coughed, his eyes streaming tears.

"I see now that I worried for nothing." Natalie leaned on her elbows and gave Molly a slow, why-you-sly-little-boots smile. "Your father obviously knew more about raising a child than I gave him credit for."

"He knew how to raise a princess," Molly corrected her. "Don't breathe a word of this to anyone, Mother."

"Not a peep." Natalie grinned, her amber brown eyes dancing. "I can hardly wait to see your uncle Karroll's face."

Molly could—forever—but there was a one-hundred-and-fifty-million-dollar deficit waiting for her on the throne, a projected shortfall of another sixty or seventy million over the next fiscal year and absolutely no other way to lift the badly crunched St. Cristobel economy out of the red and into the black *but* to sell the Phantom to the highest bidder.

"There isn't a thing Uncle Karroll can do about it," Molly said firmly. "A week from tomorrow, I'll be running the show in St. Cristobel."

Natalie gave an unladylike snort. "Since when did that ever stop Karroll Savard? He gave your father ulcers."

Bleeding ulcers that had turned cancerous and killed him four years ago, but there was no point dredging that up. Or pointing out that Natalie's demand for a divorce twelve years earlier had put as much strain on her father as the burdens of his office and the Grand Duke's endless machinations. Her mother's hatred of her ex-brother-in-law was based as much in guilt as genuine dislike. Molly knew that. She also knew Natalie was deliberately trying to change the subject.

"I can handle Uncle Karroll," she said, more bravado than confidence in her voice. "Now tell me about Chase Sanquist."

"I met him at Ascot four years ago," Natalie answered shortly. "He was filling in for his cousin Tony. Chase does that a lot. Tony's an archaeologist and spends months on end digging things up."

"And?" Molly prodded, as her mother raised her cappuccino.

"And what?" Natalie asked, her gaze narrowing over the brim of her cup.

"What does he do when he isn't standing in for his cousin?"

"Haven't a clue." Natalie drank and glanced at her diamond-banded watch. "Oops. Gotta go. I'm meeting Contessa Santella for tea in fifteen minutes."

"Otto'll be along with the Rolls," Danny said. "We'll drop you."

"I'll walk, thanks." Natalie put down her cup, slipped into her mink and winked at Molly. "I saw an Oleg Cassini two blocks back. Think I'll nip in for a closer look on my way."

"Buy a hat while you're at it," Molly suggested, watching her mother sweep her hair under the electric pink cap. "That one is definitely not you."

"Why do you think I'm wearing it? There are still people in this country who'd love to string me up for divorcing your father, God rest his soul." Natalie rose, leaned over the table and kissed Molly. "Your uncle Karroll chief among them. Take good care of my little princess, Danny."

"Always." Diello rose and helped her gather her packages. "Maybe you should let us drive you."

"Maybe you shouldn't worry." Natalie smiled and looped her shopping bags over her wrists. "Absolutely no one will recognize me in this getup."

She blew a kiss at Molly and swept away toward the exit. Molly watched her go, bending her arm over the back of her chair again. "How much do you think she wasn't telling?" she asked Danny.

"Hard to say. Natalie's one hell of a poker player," he replied. "Here's Otto. Drink up and let's go."

Just this once, while she still could, Molly wanted to stamp her foot and shout, "No!" The impulse was so strong her heart started to pound. Her days of freedom, relative as it was and always had been, were numbered—seven to be exact.

The over-the-shoulder glimpse she had of the white Rolls limo gliding up to the curb, the sun flashing on the royal seal emblazoned on the doors—the Savard coat of arms topped by a gold crown—reminded her of her duty. Throwing a tantrum wouldn't change it or delay it. Molly sighed, felt her heartbeat slow and the rebellious impulse slip away.

"Coming, Mother Diello," she said resignedly.

"Watch it, your mouthiness," he retorted unperturbed.

While she finished her cold cappuccino, Danny gathered her packages, then preceded her out of the café past the waiters and the maître d' lined up to bow to their soon-to-be sovereign. All too soon, Molly thought, dread mixing with excitement at the thought of her coronation.

She nodded to Otto as he bowed and held open the rear door of the Rolls. She slid first into the back seat, then Danny. Otto waited until he'd dumped her packages on the seat between them, then shut the door and folded himself in behind the wheel. Next to Danny, Otto was the biggest man Molly had ever seen, as fair as Diello was dark. He was a native of St. Cristobel, though natives were hard to peg.

The Rolls purred away from the curb, its left turn signal flashing. Traffic yielded to the royal limo, and Otto made a deft U-turn in the middle of Parabello Street. Danny leaned forward and opened the glass partition.

"Anything goin' on at the palace?"

"Absolute chaos." Otto grinned in the rearview mirror. His accent was as hard to peg as his looks, though he reminded Molly of Dolph Lundgren. He looked Scandinavian but spoke English like a Frenchman. "Florists and caterers and deliverymen bringing presents all over the place. You'd think the princess had never had a birthday before."

The princess wasn't listening. She sat sideways on the white leather seat watching a gray Renault retrieve the two plainclothes palace guards who followed her everywhere.

"Can you lose those guys, Otto?" Molly asked, as the Renault rocketed after the limo.

The chauffeur checked his mirror and nodded. "As Your Highness wishes," he said. The Rolls shot through the intersection of Parabello and *rue de* Savard, Otto honking the horn and signing to the gendarme. The officer nodded and dropped his baton. The gray Renault skidded to a halt, tires squealing, its driver fuming. Molly had a glimpse of his disgruntled expression as she turned around on the seat with a smile.

Otto caught her eye in the rearview mirror and winked. Molly winked back. He was the best present her father had ever given her, for her twenty-first birthday.

"Officially Otto is your chauffeur," he'd told her. "Unofficially, he's the son of an old and trusted friend, a man of great discretion with far-reaching and—well, let's just say interesting connections. Don't ask. Not ever. You can trust Otto to be discreet in the face of indiscretion and loyal to the death."

Molly trusted her father's advice and had never asked anything, up to and including Otto's last name. But she'd wondered.

"What was that for?" Danny asked, cocking an eyebrow at her.

"Flexing my royal muscles," Molly replied airily. "I'm sick and tired of being followed."

"Is that why you sorta accidentally on purpose dropped that package outside the café?"

Molly made a sheepish face. "Was I that obvious?"

"A blind guy might've missed it." Danny paused to frown at her. "*I* didn't."

"Sanquist has been following me for three days," Molly replied with a shrug. "I was curious, that's all."

Danny glowered at her. "You and the cat."

"Calm down, Dano." Molly patted his wrist. "I'm only going to dance with him."

"Damn right that's all you're gonna do," he growled. "And don't call me Dano."

Danny claimed he could still hear the Bears' fans screaming, "Drill 'em, Dano!" whenever he trotted up to the line of scrimmage in his dreams. He hated the takeoff of *Hawaii Five-0*'s "Book 'em, Dano." He wouldn't even watch the show, but Molly loved the old reruns, held her breath late at night waiting for McGarrett to utter those three little words. In Italian, with lots of snow in the picture despite the satellite dish on the roof of the palace.

Molly had been Driller Diello's biggest fan, a skinny little twelve-year-old in a cut-down mink that belonged to her mother, shivering in the stands at Soldier Field on visits with Natalie in Chicago, screaming, "Drill 'em, Dano!" until she was hoarse. She wrote him fan letters; he sent her autographed pictures. When his knee was shattered in a play-off game, her mother took her to visit him in the hospital and offered him a job.

For the past ten years Danny had been Molly's bodyguard and her best friend. In the two-hundred-and-thirty-room royal palace that covered a five-acre sprawl near the summit of what was more mountain than steep hill in the middle of San Blanco, Otto and Danny were her only friends. When Otto swept the Rolls through the gold-tipped, black iron front gates, guards in full ceremonial dress shouldered their pikes at attention.

Molly acknowledged them with a nod but really didn't see them. She was thinking, elbow bent on the armrest, chin on her fist, wondering why—if he wasn't a jewel thief—

Chase Sanquist had been following her. When she saw him in the midst of a tour group that stopped on the palace steps to watch her limo pass, she shot bolt upright on the seat.

Otto slowed the Rolls so Molly could wave to the tourists, as was her custom, but her hand froze and her breath caught when Chase Sanquist bowed alongside the tour guide and his eyes locked with hers. They were a startling shade of blue, almost sapphire, and held hers for only the moment it took the Rolls to cruise past the steps. Brief as it was, the eye contact and the amused smile lifting the corner of his mouth left her face and her fingertips tingling.

Chase Sanquist's eyes, Molly realized with a jolt, were the same color as the Phantom.

4

"THAT GUY GETS AROUND," Danny said, craning his neck to look at Chase Sanquist through the back window of the Rolls.

"Doesn't he, though?" Molly agreed, rubbing the hair standing on her arms.

What was he doing here? Casing the joint, she thought, then made a face. She'd seen one too many episodes of *Hawaii Five-0*, that was all, read one too many security reports from Inspector Francis. Or was it?

Statecraft, her father said, was two parts common sense, one part luck, and the rest pure instinct. More than once she'd seen him veto a bill or deny a petition based solely on the fact that it didn't feel right. Always, ultimately, his decisions had proven right. From watching him she'd learned to trust her hunches.

Something about Chase Sanquist didn't feel right. Every instinct Molly had said there was something very wrong about him. Big time. The question was what?

Otto swept the Rolls to a stop beneath the pillared, copper-roofed portico covering the south entrance to the palace, got out and opened Molly's door. She swung out of it and nodded at the tour group making its way toward the gate.

"Check that guy out," she said to Otto. "The tall blond one with the guide. His name is Chase Sanquist."

"Sounds like a Brit," Danny added, climbing out of the Rolls with her packages, "but I'll bet he isn't."

"I assume, Highness," Otto replied, his glance following Molly's, "that you want what's off the record as well as on."

"As always, Otto, you read my mind." Molly gave him a smile and turned with Danny as he shifted his load into one arm and opened the copper-plated palace door.

She went through it, turned and asked, "If Sanquist is a thief and intends to steal the Phantom, why do you think he made such a point of introducing himself to me?"

"I don't think he's a thief. Inspector Francis thinks he's a thief." Danny redistributed his load as they started down the wide marble corridor toward her private elevator. "I think he's a gigolo."

"Oh, Danny!" Molly laughed, fished in her bag for the key and inserted it in the slot cleverly disguised as part of the rococo wall.

Only she and Diello and Otto had keys to the elevator. The Grand Duke and the security guards who delivered the Phantom into her keeping promptly at five-thirty every day had access to her fifth-floor apartment via another bank of elevators, but this was the shortest way from the state salon in the east wing where the Phantom sat daily on display.

Her uncle had screamed bloody blue hell about security, but Molly held her ground. She'd be damned if she'd give him control of her only unguarded exit from the palace. The parliament had backed her, which infuriated her uncle but didn't surprise Molly. Next to money, privacy was the most highly valued commodity in St. Cristobel.

Still chuckling, she stepped into the car, pushed five, leaned back in the corner and spread her hands on the brass rails. Danny followed her, glowering.

"Is that why you told me to forget about his tush?" She teased. "Because you think he's a gigolo?"

"I told you to forget about his tush 'cause he's trouble. In capital letters."

"I don't know why you say that," Molly replied, feigning innocence. "He seemed perfectly nice to me."

"That's *why* he's trouble," Danny growled, as the elevator doors parted.

Molly stepped out of the car into a marble-floored alcove in the living room of her apartment. A bust of her grandfather, Caspar IV, glared at her fiercely from a goldleaf Louis XIV credenza. She hung her shoulder bag over his bald, hammered-bronze head, heard Danny sigh behind her and paper crackle as he dumped her packages on a velvet settee.

"Do I have time to skate before the guards deliver the Phantom?" she asked, turning to face him.

Danny raised an eyebrow. "Haven't you had enough exercise for one day?"

"That wasn't exercise, that was shopping. Do I have time or not?"

"'Bout an hour," he said, looking at his watch.

"Good. Wanna tag along?"

"Sure."

Molly blinked at him, surprised. Danny never wanted to go with her. "Are you going to *skate?*" She had to see this.

"Hell, no, I'm not gonna skate. My knee's had all it can take for one day. I'm gonna sit and wait for you on that nice cushy little sofa by the elevator."

"Why can't you wait for me on this nice cushy little sofa like you usually do?" Molly asked, waving her hand toward a deep-cushioned couch.

"'Cause I wouldn't be much of a bodyguard, would I?"

Molly opened her mouth, then shut it. Obviously, she wasn't the only one with a bad case of precoronation jitters.

"I'll be ready in a second," she said.

Molly went through her bedroom into the dressing room adjacent to the bathroom. She sat down on the dressing table bench, tugged off her boots and dug her Rollerblades out of the closest of her six walk-in closets. She draped them over her shoulder by their tied-together laces, stood up and blinked at her reflection in the full-length mirror on the inside of the closet door.

A good little princess would forget about skating, summon Inspector Francis and tell him she'd met the man whose name was numero uno on each and every one of his weekly watch lists. That, coupled with the fact that Chase Sanquist had been following her and his not-so-thinly veiled accusations of thievery were grounds enough under the laws of St. Cristobel to have him detained until after her coronation, until after she'd walked down the boulevard-wide center aisle of the cathedral of San Blanco with her father's crown on her head and the Phantom—her country's sure-fire ticket out of astronomical debt—blazing atop the royal scepter.

Molly about-faced, picked up the receiver of a white French telephone on an ivory inlaid ebony table and paused, shivering at the memory of Chase Sanquist's eyes smiling at her through the window of the Rolls. Were they really the same sapphire blue as the Phantom, or was her imagination working overtime?

So what if they were? It didn't mean anything. It was just coincidence. Wasn't it? Molly bit her lip, dropped the phone and adjusted her skates over her shoulder.

St. Cristobel had no jails, only the dungeons in the bowels of the mountain beneath the palace. Molly had seen them—once. The thought of throwing someone, *anyone*, into them, made her blood run cold. Besides, clapping

Chase Sanquist into rusty chains just didn't feel right. Not yet.

She'd give him a chance, but if he blew it, if he took one false step toward the Phantom, she'd lock him up and feed Danny the key for breakfast. In the meantime, she'd skate off the precoronation nerves that had her stuck in overdrive, soak in a hot tub, have dinner with her mother and Danny and veg out in front of the TV.

"Ready," she said to Diello, smiling as she entered the living room.

He pushed the call button for the elevator, held the door for her, then followed her into the car. Molly pressed one and leaned against the rail. So did Danny.

"How come you didn't tell Natalie about your original money-making scheme?" he asked.

"Since *I* didn't want to tell her anything, why would I tell her Uncle Karroll almost had a stroke when I suggested selling some of the smaller pieces of the Crown jewels? I think Mother distrusts him enough, don't you?"

"Nope. I don't think anyone does. Especially you."

"We've had this conversation, Danny," Molly retorted, stepping out of the car as the doors opened. "Uncle Karroll is my father's brother. He's also Grand Duke and Regent. I have to be careful how I handle him."

"All right, already," Danny grumbled, sitting down on a bergère-styled sofa opposite the marble bench she dropped onto to lace on her skates. "I'll keep my mouth shut and wait right here."

"You do that." Molly rose and ruffled a hand through his gray-threaded dark hair. He took a swat at her wrist and missed, like he always did, settled back and sighed as she skated away.

Molly's father had signed a royal proclamation when she was ten forbidding her to skate anywhere but on the ground floor, where the corridors were nearly thirty feet wide. It's that, he'd explained to her, or all the servants will quit.

He would have built her a skating rink if she'd asked, but she loved flying down the marble corridors, so fast the priceless antiques and treasures lining the walls and the faces in the portraits of her ancestors blurred. Skating was her only outlet, one of the few solitary things allowed her, and she cherished it as fiercely as she loved and hated being a princess.

Since her parents' divorce twelve years ago, she'd felt like a yo-yo; torn between her duty and her desires, between her father and St. Cristobel and her mother and Chicago. It had been worse since her father's death. With her coronation staring her in the face, it was nearing critical mass. Molly had been skating a lot lately, logging at least five miles a day down the avenue-wide hallways.

She started slowly, to loosen and warm her muscles. Wouldn't do to pull a hamstring and not be able to dance with Chase Sanquist tomorrow night. Molly wondered what he'd look like in a tuxedo, then pushed the thought away and concentrated on her skating.

By the time she reached the east wing where the Phantom sat on display she was flying, had worked up a comfortable sweat, felt warm and flushed and relaxed. The state salon where the Crown jewels resided by day was half-walled with bulletproof glass on the north and south.

Molly came careening around the southernmost corner into the east wing just as one of the security guards charged with transporting the collection lifted her grandmother's ruby tiara from its red velvet drape. From the corner of her eye, she saw the tiara slip out of the man's hands. When it hit the marble floor and exploded into a million red shards, Molly dove for the deck to stop herself.

Heart thudding, she spun in a half circle, her left ankle catching the leg of a Hepplewhite chair. She felt the wrench all the way up her calf and lay still, breathing hard to catch her breath, wide-eyed and thinking furiously.

Rubies did not shatter like cheap glass. Gripping the edge of the half-wainscoted wall and mindful of the throb in her ankle, Molly pulled herself slowly upward, careful to lift just her eyes above the wood edge.

The captain in charge of the detail was yelling at the guard who'd dropped the tiara. Molly couldn't hear him through the thick glass, but his jaw worked nonstop and his face was nearly purple. Two other guards were scrambling on all fours, scooping up bits of red glass with their hands.

Holy shit, Molly thought, her mother's favorite oath springing instantly into her head. Now she knew why her uncle had gone ballistic when she'd suggested selling off some of the lesser pieces of the royal collection. And why he insisted on handpicking the guards for the security details.

She didn't see the Phantom. The guards must have already transferred the royal scepter into the security cart, a heavily armored safe on wheels. Ducking below the glass, Molly pressed her back to the wainscoting and tried to think what to do. It came to her in a blinding flash of self-preservation— *Get the hell out of here before somebody sees you.*

An antique ormolu clock on a nearby credenza said it was five minutes past five. She had twenty-five minutes before the guards were supposed to deliver the Phantom. She hoped this would slow them up enough to give her time to gimp her way back to Danny, the elevator and her apartment.

Quickly unlacing her skates, Molly tied them together over her shoulder, turned on her knees the way she'd come and started crawling. Her ankle pulsed with a vengeance, and her hands left damp, clammy prints on the marble floor. She made the corner, scrambled around it and stopped, blinking at a pair of dark blue trouser legs impeccably tailored to break just at the top of two black Italian leather shoes.

Molly had never been so glad she'd hurt herself in her life. She sat back on the heels of her hands, knowing whose face she'd see before she forced herself to look up.

"Hi, Uncle Karroll," she said with a cheerful and she hoped innocent smile. "Can you give a girl with a sprained ankle a hand?"

5

THE GRAND DUKE did not look amused. Or convinced, though Molly's ankle pulsed with every beat of her heart. He looked wary and suspicious, his gaze flicking over her head toward the turn in the corridor before settling firmly — and searchingly, Molly thought — on her face.

"What are you doing here, Marguerite?" Karroll Savard stretched a hand down to her. "You're supposed to be in your apartment to receive the Phantom."

"I would be if I could crawl faster," Molly said, taking his hand and levering herself up on her right foot.

She tried to pull away then, but her uncle held her fast. An angry frown all but swallowed his clipped dark mustache peppered with gray.

"This is the very reason I forbade you to skate until after your coronation. I will not have you limping onto the throne and embarrassing us both in front of the whole of St. Cristobel."

"Not to mention the film crew from CNN," Molly replied flippantly.

Her uncle's frown and the ruddy flush above his snowy, starched shirt collar deepened. Molly glared at him, not quite eye to eye but close. None of the Savards were very tall, Karroll barely five-nine, though he appeared taller in a pin-striped navy suit. Molly was five-six like her mother.

"Which ankle did you sprain?" Karroll asked, glancing swiftly downward as he abruptly let go of her hand.

Thrown off balance, Molly stumbled onto her left foot and winced as a sliver of pain sliced up her leg. "My left," she snapped, flinging her hand against the wall to brace herself. "As you can plainly see."

Her uncle's gaze lifted and he smiled. Not with relish at her pain, Molly thought, but relief that the sprain was genuine.

"Sit here and I'll ring for the royal physician." He tried to guide her toward a close by blue velvet bench, but Molly wrenched free.

"I can hobble that far on my own," she said, leaning on the wall and hopping on her right foot.

"This is your mother's doing. Disaster falls every time she visits. Rollerblading may be marvelous exercise for a fashion model, but not for a princess."

"*Ex*-fashion model," Molly corrected him sharply. "Now CEO of Vincennes Meat Packing. Named Chicago's businesswoman of the year for pulling Grandad's company out of chapter eleven and turning a two-million-dollar deficit into a five-million-dollar profit in three years."

"Single-handedly, of course," Karroll replied acidly. "When she wasn't skiing in St. Moritz or shopping in Paris."

Molly heard footsteps behind her and bit back an equally nasty retort. A princess didn't scream at people—though God knew she'd love to—especially where any of the three hundred plus servants and guards might overhear. Tabloid headlines like Princess Slugs Uncle were not good p.r. She looked over her shoulder and saw Danny, not a footman, ambling toward them around the corridor turn. She couldn't remember ever being so glad to see him.

"Took another header, huh?" he asked mildly, his bass voice echoing off the marble walls.

"Sort of," Molly replied, easing herself onto the bench. "I twisted my ankle."

"This is your fault, Diello." Karroll Savard rounded on him angrily. "You are *supposed* to be Marguerite's bodyguard."

"Don't get your shorts in a snuggie, Your Grace," Danny replied unperturbed. "A round of contrast baths and an ice bag and she'll be fine by morning."

"We'll see what the royal physician says about that."

"I don't need Dr. Albrecht," Molly objected. "Danny's forgotten more about sports medicine than he'll ever know."

"Yeah, and I've got the scars to prove it." Diello glowered at the Grand Duke as if he'd like to give him a couple just to prove the point.

He ignored Danny as he always did, his gaze lifting from Molly's face toward the corridor turn again. Absently, he twisted the signet ring on the little finger of his left hand.

"Very well, for the moment. Return to your apartment, Marguerite. I'm sure the guards are waiting to deliver the Phantom."

"They're running late," Danny told him. "I came to see why."

The Grand Duke's gaze flashed to Danny's face, a muscle in his jaw beating visibly. "The Crown jewels are not your concern, Diello."

"Or yours, either, Your Grace." Danny smiled broadly. "Not for much longer, anyway."

Molly watched her uncle swallow, hard, to control his temper, then square his shoulders at Danny. There was a flicker of something else besides fury in his eyes, but she couldn't decide what.

"Take Marguerite upstairs," he commanded. "I'll see to the guards and the Phantom."

Danny nodded, stepping aside as the Grand Duke strode past him. When he disappeared around the corner into the east wing, Danny crossed the six feet of marble floor separating him from Molly and scooped her off the bench. His right arm circling her shoulders, his left hooked beneath her knees, he bore her swiftly down the corridor toward her private elevator.

"We got trouble," Molly said shakily, looping one arm around his neck and clutching her skates with the other.

"Not here. Save it till we get upstairs."

Molly did, biting her lip to keep from blurting out what she'd seen. There were bugs and cameras all over the palace, except in her apartment, where the security grid rendered them redundant.

Since the Phantom had yet to be delivered, they didn't have to fool with the intricate bypass system to deactivate the hologram field. Less than two minutes after he'd swooped her off the bench, Danny lowered Molly onto the sofa in the living room, went down on his knees in front of her and swung her feet into his lap.

"Which ankle?"

"Left," she said, sweeping off her cap and gripping his shoulders as he peeled off her socks. "One of the guards dropped my grandmother's ruby tiara. It shattered when it hit the floor."

"That explains why I saw them crawling around." Danny cupped her heel in his hand and glanced up at her. "Rubies don't break that easily, do they?"

"No."

"I didn't think so. What d'you think?"

"I think I know why Uncle Karroll almost stroked out when I suggested selling smaller pieces of the collection. Someone's been removing the real stones and replacing them with fakes. If it isn't Uncle Karroll, I'll eat my crown. What I don't know is why."

"Put Otto on it. He'll find out. What happened?"

Molly told him between gasps and winces as Danny probed her ankle gently but expertly. "Uncle Karroll caught me crawling out of the east wing," she finished. "He didn't believe I'd sprained my ankle. If he *is* stealing the jewels, as soon as the guards tell him they broke the tiara, he'll suspect I saw it happen."

"Suspect, hell." Danny pulled the ottoman closer and swung her left leg onto it. "He'll *know*."

"So how much trouble am I in?"

"How much are *we* in," Danny corrected her, getting to his feet. "A shit load, kiddo. Up to our ears."

"Get Otto up here." Molly swung her foot to the floor and braced her hands on the arm of the sofa. "Fast. Then get me—"

"Down, girl." Danny pushed her back as she started to rise. "First we take care of your ankle so you can dance with your gigolo tomorrow night, then I get Otto up here. Maybe Inspector Francis, too. Maybe he—"

A knock on the paneled, double mahogany doors interrupted him. "Your Highness!" a muffled voice called. "It is Captain Maxmillian and the security detail."

"Just a moment, Captain!" Molly called. Then she said to Danny, "Get me my slippers. Then use my private phone and call Otto."

"Can you make it to your chair?"

"No problem."

Danny nodded and headed for her bedroom. Hopping from one piece of furniture to the next, Molly made her way to a massive red velvet gilt armchair with a matching footstool. As chairs went, it was more like a throne. Molly sat in it every day at five-thirty to accept the Phantom and the rest of the Crown jewels for their nightly safekeeping, just like her father had done, and her grandfather and every Savard ruler of St. Cristobel since 1752.

The ritual was begun by Sandor I, Crown Prince of Paranoia, who'd trusted absolutely no one absolutely. Historians suspected he'd had syphilis, which Molly thought was a convenient cop-out for the fact that he was a psychopath.

One of the first things she planned to do as Crown princess was do away with the ritual of the jewel transfer. She planned to have better things to do with her time.

Danny came out of her bedroom, tossed her a pair of hot pink slipper socks with gripper soles and waited while she put them on. When Molly nodded, he opened the doors and admitted six bowing guards—Captain Maxmillian, the man she'd seen shouting at the clumsy guard, two others pushing the heavily armored and triple-locked gray steel safe containing the jewels between them, and four more packing nine-millimeter pistols. The man who'd dropped the tiara was not among them.

"Highness." The captain bowed low in front of Molly. "We are returning your treasures into your keeping, having protected them this day with our very lives for the glory of St. Cristobel."

More tradition than ceremony, the words he spoke were as old as the jewels themselves. Molly replied with her part of the daily ritual, "We are grateful, Captain, for your courage and that of your men in safeguarding the wealth of St. Cristobel. Pray show us our treasures."

Except for my grandmother's ruby tiara, she thought, certain that she knew how Captain Maxmillian would explain its absence and how her uncle had been robbing St. Cristobel. The captain didn't look like a traitor, not that Molly was sure she'd recognize one, but he did look extremely nervous, a sheen of perspiration on his forehead as he straightened.

"All the jewels are here save one, Highness. The ruby tiara of the Princess Consort Alistrina. The lord chamberlain found certain of the stones to be loose, judged the tiara in need of repair and ordered it removed for that purpose."

So late I get so smart, Molly thought furiously. "You have certification from the lord chamberlain and His Grace the Regent so stating?" she asked.

"I do, Highness." The captain snapped his fingers for a clipboard carried by one of the armed guards and gave it to her with a gold ballpoint pen.

As Molly took them, Danny came back from the bedroom and gave her a discreet nod. She acknowledged it with one of her own that looked like it was directed at Captain Maxmillian and turned her attention to the clipboard.

In the four years since her father's death, she'd signed at least a score of such authorization sheets for the repair or cleaning of certain pieces of the collection. She tried to remember if she'd signed one for the royal scepter but couldn't. She'd check, of course, but knew she'd have to be damn careful.

Signing her full name beneath her uncle's and that of the lord chamberlain, Molly handed the clipboard back to Captain Maxmillian. He breathed an audible sigh—relieved that he still had his head, Molly thought—and backed away as Danny came forward to help her up.

Leaning on his arm, Molly made her halting way to the massive fireplace flanked by matching baroque cupboards and intricate rococo walls. As she pressed the gold-leaf navel of a cherub plucking a harp on the mantel facing, the right-hand cupboard slid aside to reveal a vault that would bring tears to a Swiss banker's eyes. Molly worked the combinations on all four locks, hopped aside and let Danny open the six-foot-thick steel door.

Her uncle knew the combinations, too, for all the good it would do him once the grid was up. The tiniest flicker in the field would bring an army of palace guards boiling into her apartment within seconds. It was Molly's only consolation.

This has to be how it's done, she thought, watching the guards transfer the jewels from the cart to the vault. The switch is made when the stones are removed for maintenance. The real ones leave, the fakes come back.

"Highness." Bowing, Captain Maxmillian offered her a white velvet cushion. "The royal scepter."

The Phantom winked at Molly like a giant blue eye from the crown piece of the eighteen-inch-long scepter. It was the size of Danny's fist, dwarfing the other stones surrounding it and those crusting the gold and platinum staff in size and brilliance. It was also the same color as Chase Sanquist's eyes. Molly was sure of it. Well, almost.

"Give me a hand here, would you, Dano?"

He took the cushion from Captain Maxmillian and followed her as she limped into the vault. When he slid the pillow onto its shelf, Molly leaned over it and peered at the Phantom.

"What do you think?" she whispered, though they were well out of earshot of the guards. "Real or fake?"

"Beats me. I suggest you ask an expert. Like Inspector Francis."

"I would, if Uncle Karroll hadn't hired him." Molly leaned her elbow on the shelf, gazed into the fiery blue depths of the Phantom and tapped her little finger against the corner of her mouth. "What I need is an independent expert, someone I know I can trust."

"Forget Gerard and Anton, then," Danny said, referring to the royal jewelers. "Somebody there's gotta be in on this scam. Otto can find you someone."

If anybody could it was Otto, but Molly suddenly had a better idea. It came to her in a blinding flash of sapphire-blue facets.

"Never mind Otto." She glanced with a smile at Danny. "I'll ask Chase Sanquist."

He blinked at her, twice. "Did you hit your head when you fell?"

"He has a vested interest in the Phantom, Dano. It's as important to him to make sure it's real as it is to me."

"Hell, yes, it is—he's a jewel thief."

"*You* said he's a gigolo."

"Yeah, but what if I'm wrong?"

"Then who better to tell me if this is the real Phantom or a cubic zirconium?"

"Or to steal it right out from under your nose."

"That'll be a little tough to do from the dungeon, Dano."

"That's my girl." He grinned. "But don't call me Dano." He helped her out of the vault, shut the door and spun the locks.

When Molly pushed the cherub's navel, the wall slid noiselessly back into place. When Danny switched on the crystal lamp on the table beside the velvet chair, the security grid shimmered to life.

The fireplace wall seemed a foot closer than it really was. Other sections of wall moved closer or farther away. Every three months the system was reprogrammed to change the holographs. Four times a year Molly and Danny and Otto crept around the apartment on eggshells until they'd memorized the perimeters.

"Thank you, Captain Maxmillian," Molly said formally. "Your duty is discharged. You may leave us."

The guards bowed and followed Danny to the doors. He opened them on Otto, his hand raised to knock. Danny ushered him in, the guards out, shut and locked the doors.

"I'm going to enjoy throwing Captain Maxmillian into the dungeon. Right next to the lord chamberlain and Uncle Karroll," she said, as she dropped into the red velvet chair, swung her pulsing ankle on the footstool and looked at Otto. "What have you got on Chase Sanquist?"

"The dossier Inspector Francis keeps on him," Otto replied, sweeping off his uniform cap, "links Mr. Sanquist to the dates and sites of several major jewel thefts in Europe, the Orient and the Middle East during the past twelve years. So, coincidentally, do the dates on his passport. He's an American citizen but has no criminal record, not even a parking ticket."

"Looks like I was wrong," Danny said, catching her eye as he arched a dark, shaggy brow. "You thinkin' what I'm thinkin'?"

"You bet I am." Molly bent her elbow on the arm of her chair and looked steadily at Danny. "If the Phantom hasn't been switched, and Uncle Karroll hasn't already beaten me to it, I'm going to hire Chase Sanquist to steal it."

Then she sighed, closed her eyes and rubbed the bridge of her nose where the beginnings of a headache pulsed. The pain was a piercing, blue-white light behind her eyelids.

Its name was the Phantom.

6

A SIMILAR IMAGE of blazing blue-white light flickered through Chase's mind, but it wasn't at all painful. It was glorious, orgasmic, more beautiful than the purple and mauve spears of sunset shooting through the storm clouds gathering on the horizon as he made his way from the palace along Parabello Street toward the bay.

It was the Phantom.

His birthright, his destiny. Maybe his Waterloo, but he didn't think so. It didn't feel like the end of the line, it felt like the beginning. A threshold, a doorway to something beyond his imagining. It pulsed through his veins like a drug, heady and wondrous, a sensation so strong it had yet to leave him, though he'd torn himself away from the glass protecting the stone and staring, mesmerized, into its bottomless blue-white facets the better part of an hour ago.

He'd seen a lot of rocks in his time, but nothing like the Phantom. He knew everything there was to know about it, had memorized every word ever written about it, studied every photograph ever taken of it—none of which had prepared him for the impact of laying eyes on it.

Or the realization that a fair number of the stones in the smaller pieces of the St. Cristobel Crown jewels were paste. He wondered if Her Serene Highness knew, if that's how she financed her shopping sprees.

The only man capable of crafting such superb fakes was Jean-Marc DuValle, an old friend of his uncle Cosmo. His front business was an antique shop in San Blanco's old harbor district, lately made fashionable—at least until the sun went down—by extensive renovations along the water-front.

DuValle's clientele included the lesser nobility and nouveau riche of St. Cristobel, a stratum of society that seemed to be chronically in need of cash. An interesting coincidence if you believed in such things. Chase didn't.

He believed in the slow warning crawl up the back of his neck as he crossed an empty square that opened to the bay on one side. The cobblestones underfoot were artfully mired to look centuries old. So were the Victorian street lamps flickering to life amid ice-cream tables and locked-for-the-night fast-food stalls. Wisps of mist hung around their frosted globes, along with the smell of old grease and the certainty that someone was following him.

Someone usually was, so he wasn't surprised. He paused beneath a street lamp and lighted a cigarette from the pack he carried and sometimes smoked, using the nicotine rush to boost his senses.

A hard-soled shoe like those worn by plainclothes palace guards scraped stone behind him to the right, and on his left a shadowy figure faded into the blackness of an alley. In the reflection of the street lamp on a shop window, Chase saw a flash of white, probably a scarf.

He tossed his cigarette away and moved on, his senses laser sharp on full alert. He cut diagonally across the square into a narrow street that corkscrewed up a hill, his shadows hanging well behind him. DuValle's shop lay a darkening half block away in the pooled light of the display window trapped beneath the awning.

Chase slipped past the door, reaching behind him for the English and French open sign. He flipped it over and eased the door shut—so smoothly that the brass bell, hung by a hair-trigger wire, never moved. It hadn't since Chase was seventeen.

The small, treasure-crammed shop smelled of old wood and even older dust. It was mostly dark, except for the light in the window and the jeweled reflections cast by the Tiffany lamp at Jean-Marc DuValle's right elbow. He smiled without looking up, rainbow prisms gleaming on his headful of silver hair and the gold fountain pen scratching across the blue-lined pages of a fat ledger.

"Turn the lock and prepare the tea," he said in French. "I'll be with you in a moment."

Chase did as instructed, depositing his camera and light meter on a leather-topped drum table new since his last visit before brewing a pot of Darjeeling in a Wedgwood pot once used by Queen Victoria. Jean-Marc was an unabashed royalist. He put out cups, one of which matched the pot, then sat in a Queen Anne chair.

DuValle did business with no one, not even the nephew of his oldest friend, until he'd drunk tea with them and smoked their cigarettes. Chase took out a lighter and an unopened pack of unfiltered Camels, Jean-Marc's preferred brand. Chase preferred not to smoke at all, but he'd learned.

He'd learned a lot of things from Cosmo, things he probably would've learned from his father if he'd lived to teach him. Then again, maybe not. Both Phillip and Linda Sanquist had been certain that reclaiming the Phantom would make that unnecessary. Chase used to wonder how different his life might have been if they'd lived. He hadn't thought about it in a long time, hadn't a clue why he was now.

"You're late." Jean-Marc capped his pen, closed the ledger and rose from a shot-pocked campaign desk Napoléon had abandoned on the Russian steppes. "I expected you four years ago when the Crown Prince died."

"Corpses don't carry royal scepters." Chase peeled cellophane tape off the pack and smiled. "Live princesses do."

"Be wary of this one, this Marie-Marguerite. She is more than she seems." DuValle crossed the shop and perched on the arm of a hooded leather chair beside the table. "They say even her uncle the Regent tiptoes around her."

"Do they?" Chase lighted two cigarettes and passed him one with a cup of Darjeeling. "And what do you say?"

"She is a woman. A Savard, true enough, but sooner or later she will be foolish." DuValle held his saucer on one knee, dragged on his cigarette and smiled. "Perhaps she already has. Only a fool would have let you walk out of the palace. Or a woman."

"Shame on you, Jean-Marc." Chase tsked, the harsh smoke burning his nose. "Who minds the shop while you're out snooping?"

"I can snoop, as you put it, shine my shoes and dance a jig while I mind my shop," DuValle proclaimed, which Chase well knew. Any expert fence and forger could, or he didn't last long. Jean-Marc had been in the business nearly twice as long as Chase had been alive.

"Shame on you, Chase." He pronounced his name *Chaise*, a twinkle in his gray eyes. "How could you taunt those poor guards? They were so upset they dropped a tiara from the royal collection and broke all the rubies."

"Is it here?" Chase pushed his cup away and leaned forward eagerly. "Can I see it?"

"*Mon Dieu, non,* it is not here." DuValle stiffened, genuinely affronted. "I would not stoop to such duplicity in my own country."

"If you aren't doing the forgeries, who is?"

"Gerard and Anton, for twenty-five percent off the top," he replied with a derisive snort. "Such vultures give honest thieves like us a bad name."

"The royal jewelers," Chase said thoughtfully. "That's a big-time scandal if it gets out."

"I was approached, of course." DuValle tapped the ash off his cigarette in a brass ashtray and sipped his tea. "But I told the Grand Duke, as they say in the American movies, I have to live in this town."

Chase put out his cigarette next to DuValle's. He was glad the princess wasn't ripping off her own country. The idea of anyone with eyes like hers being an embezzler left a bad taste in his mouth. So did the realization that he'd even noticed her eyes. He washed both away with a healthy swallow of Darjeeling.

"I told His Grace the same thing." DuValle paused, exhaling a stream of blue smoke that curled around his head like a wreath. "When he asked me to fence the Phantom."

Seven generations of breeding gave Chase nerves steady enough not to drop the cup rumored to have touched the lips of Anastasia, daughter of Czar Nicholas the Second. But just barely.

"When did he approach you?"

"A few weeks ago." DuValle drained his cup, set it aside and capped his hands over his knees. "Time, he said, was of the essence."

Even more so now, Chase thought, with the princess' coronation a bare week away. He wanted to leap up and pace the floor, but didn't. Instead, he cradled the delicate china cup between his hands and leaned back in his chair.

"You were smart to say no, Jean-Marc."

"You don't live as long as I have by being stupid." DuValle refilled his cup, eyeing Chase soberly through the thin curl of steam wafting from the spout of Queen Victoria's teapot. "Or by fencing cursed stones."

"I wondered when you'd get around to this." Chase put his cup down and nodded at a cuckoo clock ticking on the wall. "Ten whole minutes. Remarkable restraint, Jean-Marc."

"Don't mock me, boy," DuValle retorted in stiff, haughty French. "I have forgotten more about jewels than you will ever know."

"How many times has Cosmo called you?"

"Only once. He asked me to give you something." DuValle picked up his cup, rose and started toward Napoléon's desk. "I have been holding it for many years."

"In a minute." Chase went to the window and looked out, standing in shadow enough that he could see but not be seen. The street was clear. For the moment, anyway. He turned to Jean-Marc. "What's the Grand Duke gotten himself into besides trouble up to his neck?"

"Very unwise and under-the-table loans." DuValle sat down, cup on the desk, elbows braced on the saber-scarred lid. "Always the Grand Duke has been a big fish in a little pond, his aspirations for St. Cristobel far exceeding those of his brother and the parliament. The Soviet breakup and his position as regent gave him the opportunity to fulfill St. Cristobel's destiny as a major economic power.

"He gave money to every little country who came begging, dreaming of trade concessions and being proclaimed savior. Millions to people who have never had so much as a sou in their pocket and no idea how to care for themselves, let alone govern a country."

DuValle paused to sip his tea. The cuckoo slid out of his clock, chirping the hour to the tinny strains of Wagner. It was good and dark outside now, helped by the storm spreading like an ink stain across the sky. All the easier to pick out shadows where none should be.

"Let me guess." Chase walked to Jean-Marc, leaned against a Chippendale sideboard that faced the desk and folded his arms. "When the loans defaulted he started stealing stones from the royal collection."

"Exactly, which only dug his grave deeper. I saw no way out for him, but a miracle occurred. The duke was rescued by a sheikh named Shehabi. The name is perhaps familiar?"

Chase had pulled a few jobs in the Middle East, a very rich but dangerous paradise, where security was still mostly big guys with beards and curved swords. *Very* big guys and *very* sharp swords. He remembered the shadow he'd seen in the square and the flutter of white. Not a scarf, but a burnoose, he thought. "Surely not *that* Shehabi," he said.

"A direct descendant of the sultan from whom Sir Ossric took the Phantom." Jean-Marc took a blue satin box and a rolled parchment tied with a blue ribbon out of a side drawer and placed it on the desk next to his cup. "Before he lopped off his head."

"Don't tell me," Chase said, wishing he believed in coincidence. "When the duke couldn't repay his loans, Shehabi demanded the Phantom."

"Naturally, since it's what he wanted all along. So now the duke must steal the stone before his niece ascends the throne and he loses access to the collection granted him as regent."

"Who's he hired to do it?"

"Your friend and colleague Alec Tremayne. He was here this afternoon."

"Colleague, yes—friend, the same day hell freezes over," Chase retorted. Thorn in the side was more like it. "What did he want?"

"The usual, to brag and to gloat. To tell me exactly how he plans to steal the Phantom. Would you like to know what he said?"

"Not especially," Chase replied, his mind busily weaving these new threads together. "Tremayne doesn't worry me."

"Perhaps he should. He had a gun, very big and flashy. Lots of chrome."

No self-respecting thief carries a gun, Cosmo said, unless he wants to be a thug. Or, as in Tremayne's case, he was born one.

"Did he threaten you?"

"Tremayne threatens everyone and trusts no one. Not even the duke, so they are—how do you say—a match made by the devil. He demanded the name of my contact in the palace, demanded that I verify the security information provided him by the duke. I refused. He left in a huff."

DuValle shrugged and reached for his teacup. As he did, the sleeve of his green cardigan sweater slid up his arm, revealing four ugly, finger-shaped bruises on the old, paper-thin skin on the inside of his wrist.

Chase said nothing. To notice, let alone comment, would insult Jean-Marc. Instead, he filed the bruises as a debt Tremayne owed him—in spades—and said, "I don't suppose you'd tell me who your man is in the palace. I've always wondered."

"Suffice it to say," DuValle replied, smiling as he replaced his cup in its saucer, "that there has been a DuValle in service to every Savard ruler of St. Cristobel since they found the Phantom and came to power."

"They no more *found* it," Chase shot back, "than old Sir Ossric."

"Ah," DuValle said softly, leaning forward on his elbows. "So you *do* know the old stories."

"Sure, I know them. They make great copy for tourist brochures, but that doesn't mean I believe them."

"Perhaps this will convince you. Cosmo thought it might."

DuValle picked up the blue box and held it out to him. Chase straightened off the sideboard, took it and opened it.

On a bed of white satin lay a brooch like those worn by Scotsmen to hold their plaid at the shoulder. Two lions with tangled gold manes reared and snarled on crossed shields bisected by a claymore. It was the Sanquist coat of arms, the shield halves and the sword hilt crusted with brilliant sapphire diamonds. About eight carats worth of chips and baguettes.

Chase knew by the catch of his breath and the clutch in his gut that they were bits and pieces of the Phantom.

7

CHASE COULD FEEL his heart hammering in his chest and Jean-Marc watching him intently. He wanted to, tried to, but couldn't pull his gaze away from the brooch.

"Where in hell," he managed dazedly, "did you get this?"

"It was commissioned by Crown Prince Sandor the First, when the Phantom was recut to fit the royal scepter. He offered it to Chastain Sanquist when he came to St. Cristobel to claim the stone. It is, of course, worth a king's ransom."

And then some, Chase thought, tracing the carved gold edge with his thumbnail. There was a name for the intricate platinum inlays, for the technique that was now a lost art. He knew what it was but couldn't think of it. All he could do was stare.

"Sanquist laughed in his face, of course, and the rest, as they say, is history."

"That's right, Jean-Marc, history." Chase closed his eyes and managed to lift his head. He'd had to do the same thing in the palace to tear himself away from the Phantom. "Not legends and fairy tales."

"Look at yourself," DuValle said angrily. "You can hardly bear not to look at it. Even though it contains only tiny pieces of the Phantom. It was the same with Cosmo when I gave the brooch to him. When he could, he gave it back."

"*He what?*" Chase managed, just barely, not to shout.

"He gave it back," DuValle repeated. "And told me to destroy it."

Chase drew a quick, shallow breath, but didn't look at the brooch. He was stunned and he was furious, but he'd be damned if he'd give Jean-Marc the satisfaction. Hell, *yes*, all he could do was gawk. All the millions he'd stolen for Glyco, that bottomless, money-sucking pit he was lucky he saw twice a year. All the risks he'd taken, his father, too, and Cosmo—

Dread—cold, sick and sudden—flooded Chase. "When did you give this to Cosmo?"

"I do not recall." DuValle shrugged and reached for his teacup. "It was many years ago."

Before he could lift it from the saucer, Chase slapped the brooch down on the desk, reached across it, grabbed a fistful of sweater and hauled DuValle to his feet. Queen Victoria's cup flew out of his hand and shattered against a bookcase filled with Conan Doyle first editions.

"You've never forgotten a goddamn thing in your goddamn life, Jean-Marc."

"It was 1978," DuValle snapped. "Do you want the date and the time?"

After his parents died, not before. Relief eased Chase's grip. So did a rush of shame for even thinking such a thing, and the realization that he was behaving like a thug. Like Tremayne.

"No." He let go, gently, of DuValle and picked up the parchment.

It was very old, very thin and spattered with rusty stains. Chase untied the ribbon, carefully unrolled it and translated the not-quite-modern French written in spidery copperplate script as he read.

"Be it known to all men in all Nations that I, Crown Prince Sandor the First, ruler by might and divinity of St. Cristobel, do hereby bestow upon our beloved cousin Chastain Sanquist a brooch of sapphire diamonds bearing the heraldic crest of his family. Be it further known that for love of us and the sake of peace between us the Lord of Glyco does willfully renounce all claims to the great diamond known as Le Fantôme du St. Cristobel.

"To this writ and proclamation we both set our hand and seal this seventeenth day of April in the year of our Lord seventeen hundred and eighty-six."

There was only one seal, the wax crumbling at the edges but mostly intact. It was the royal coat of arms topped by a crown. Only the name Savard was readable in the single bold signature. The rest had smeared in whatever had splashed, long ago, on the parchment. It took Chase a minute to realize the rusty stains were old, dried blood. Chastain Sanquist's, he thought, his mouth suddenly dry.

Chase raised his head and looked at DuValle, standing behind the desk rubbing his chest. "Did Cosmo tell you to destroy this, too?"

"He does not know it exists. Only recently did it come into my possession. At last, I thought, the Sanquists have the proof they need to claim the Phantom. I will give the parchment and the brooch to Chase, so he will not have to risk his life as his father did. Then Shehabi came to St. Cristobel, for the skiing, he said, and my great plan shattered like that old cup."

That irreplaceable old cup. DuValle let his gaze drift, sadly, toward the puddle of tea and shards of bone china glittering in the lamplight.

He walked to the drum table, took down another cup and saucer from a shelf and filled it. Chase carefully rolled the parchment and tied the ribbon, put it on the sideboard, then picked up the pieces of china and wiped up the tea with his handkerchief. What in hell was wrong with him? He hadn't let his temper get the best of him since he'd bloodied Tony's nose in a squabble over a girl when he was fifteen.

"Shehabi is very rich and powerful enough to keep his presence here out of the newspapers." DuValle lighted a Camel and carried it to his desk with his tea. "He is also very patient. He sits like a vulture in a villa above the bay with seventy-five bodyguards—his closest kinsmen—and four of his wives. He skis and he smiles and he waits."

Chase wrapped the broken cup in his handkerchief and laid it on top of the bookcase. "For how long?"

"Three months."

"Give or take eight hundred years." Chase made a fist of his left hand and rubbed his knuckles across his chin.

He needed to shave, and he needed to get the hell out of St. Cristobel. He wondered if Sir Ossric had felt the same urge to clear out of Palestine in 1192 after he'd beheaded Shehabi's ancestor and namesake and stolen the Phantom.

"Maybe," Chase said slowly, "you should tell me what Tremayne said."

"He plans to hijack the royal carriage on its way to the palace, when the princess will have the scepter. He will drive the coach to the airport where a Learjet will be waiting, and take the princess along as insurance."

"He's taken hostages before," Chase said.

He didn't say that Tremayne shot them afterward, that he was wanted in France for killing a bank security guard. If Jean-Marc didn't already know, he might tell his contact, and that would tighten palace security. He decided to wait until he was safely out of St. Cristobel with the Phantom, just in case Tremayne hung around to console himself with the rest of the Crown jewels. If Diello was half as good a bodyguard as he'd been a defensive end, the princess had nothing to fear.

"Back up to the broken ruby tiara," Chase said. "Who else knows about it?"

"The lord chamberlain, the duke, the princess and her bodyguard." DuValle drew on his cigarette. "Her Highness saw the guards break it. And the duke knows she saw them."

"How close is your contact to the princess?"

"Close enough to be of assistance should difficulties arise," DuValle replied confidently.

"Inspector Francis?"

"No. The duke hired him, so the princess does not trust him."

A break at last, the only one he'd had so far. With palace guards and Shehabi's kinsmen already on his tail, the last thing Chase needed was Scotland Yard.

"If you fax the parchment to Tony," DuValle suggested, "perhaps an injunction—"

"There isn't time. Eight hundred years and three months is about the limit of anyone's patience, even an Arab's."

Chase realized he was pacing and stopped, his back to Jean-Marc. He'd been in tighter spots than this and gotten out with whatever he'd come for. He'd never left empty-handed in his life and he wasn't about to now. *Especially* now.

"'Hear me, Allah, great God of my fathers, at this, the hour of my death,'" DuValle said, the cuckoo ticking counterpoint to his quiet voice. "'Grant me peace and life eternal, and to this Infidel, murderer of thy children and thief of thy Great Eye, grant to him and his sons, and the sons of his sons, so long as the stars wheel in the sky, every wish their hearts desire.'"

"Sultan Shehabi's curse." Chase shook off the chill it gave him, the chill he felt every time he heard it, and turned with a smile. "Pretty tame stuff, I've always thought, but I suppose with Sir Ossric's sword hanging over his head he was a little pressed for time."

"Diamonds are crystals of pure carbon." DuValle stubbed out his cigarette in an ashtray Chase couldn't see over the top of the desk. "They are formed at great depths below the surface by forces of immense heat and pressure. If the energy stored in a stone the size of the Phantom could be released, the explosion would wreck the world."

"I know, Jean-Marc." Chase kept his irritation and the urgency he felt to be gone out of his voice. He'd stayed longer than he'd intended, could almost feel his shadows growing impatient—and closer, along with the faint rumble of faraway thunder. "Cosmo didn't make me study geology at Cambridge for nothing."

"From your studies, then, you know why a diamond feels cold when first you pick it up, until its high thermal conductivity absorbs the warmth of your body." DuValle rose from Bonaparte's desk, picked up the brooch and the parchment from the sideboard and brought them to Chase. "Remember what I taught you—never believe a diamond loves you because it warms to your touch."

"Cosmo says the same thing—about women."

DuValle chuckled. "A wise man, my old friend Cosmo."

"So are you, Jean-Marc. I'm sorry about the cup. I'll replace it." DuValle shrugged. *"De rien,"* he said. *It is nothing.*

Chase gave his shoulder a quick, warm clasp, then moved past him to retrieve his photo equipment from the drum table.

"There are many wise people in the world," DuValle said behind him. "Some who believe that like body heat, diamonds absorb everything around them. Thoughts and actions as well has energy. Particularly psychic energy."

"Like revenge and hatred and a dying man's curse?" Chase draped the Nikon and light meter around his neck and arched an eyebrow at Jean-Marc. "Any of these people named Shirley Maclaine?"

"One of them is Jean-Marc DuValle," he declared, lifting his chin defiantly. "The world is full of mysteries, ancient puzzles that we may never solve. We do not know who built Stonehenge and how, or the pyramids of Gaza. We can only theorize. Perhaps they found a way to tap the energy stored in diamonds."

"You mean magic?" Chase asked, his eyebrow sliding up another notch.

"Perhaps. Isn't that what we call things we don't understand?"

"Let me tell you what I understand, Jean-Marc. The princess knows I'm here and she knows who I am. So does Shehabi. There's a guy in a burnoose waiting for me outside, and at least one plainclothes palace guard."

"So." DuValle smiled, a glint of amusement crinkling the corners of his gray eyes. "It is hell to be popular."

"That's one word for it." Chase took the brooch out of its box, which was too bulky and too obvious to carry.

Tucked behind the clasp was a small square of paper. He unfolded it and read: "One teaspoon salt, one teaspoon baking soda to every eight ounces of water. Dissolve and soak for one hour."

"What's this?" he asked Jean-Marc.

"It is a recipe for a simple ionic solution to clean diamonds and rid them of negative energy."

"More magic." Chase smiled, slipped the brooch into his pants pocket and the parchment in his shirt so it wouldn't crush. He thought, as he walked to the door and looked back at DuValle with one hand on the knob, that a love potion for the princess might do him more good. "Lock up and wish me luck, Jean-Marc. I'm off to dance with a princess."

8

CHASE DIDN'T BELIEVE in magic, but he did believe history repeated itself. Time was a pendulum that swung back and forth, replaying events until it got them right.

Like the date April 17. He'd seen it two other places before he'd read it on Crown Prince Sandor I's proclamation—cut in stone on Chastain Sanquist's marker in the family mausoleum at Glyco, and printed in gilt script on Tony's invitation to the princess' birthday ball.

Chase didn't believe in coincidence, but he did believe in fate. A flawed and very selective belief system, but it worked. When he reached the square he'd crossed earlier, living proof stepped out of an alleyway about ten yards ahead of him—a big guy in a burnoose.

A *very* big guy—about six-four, two hundred and forty pounds, Chase figured—with a scimitar he withdrew from the folds of the loose silk robe he wore over an Italian suit. The curved blade gleamed in the light of a close-by street lamp. So did a gold tooth in his mouth as he smiled and tapped the blade gently against his cupped palm.

Chase stopped and reached into his pocket. In close quarters a lighter made a dandy weapon, especially when your opponent wore enough silk to make a parachute. But instead of his cigarettes, his fingers closed on the brooch; he'd left his pack and his lighter in DuValle's shop.

He was just wondering how fast two hundred and forty pounds could run when Alec Tremayne stepped out of the alley and took a spread-footed stance in front of the swordsman. He wore black jeans and boots, a black leather biker jacket and enough oil on his dark hair to lube a Mack truck.

"'Allo, Chase," Tremayne said, arms folded across his chest, the East End of London thick in his voice.

"Hello, Alec." Chase rubbed the brooch with his thumb and considered his options.

"Achmed gave you a turn, did he?"

"For a five count or so, yeah." Chase stuck to good old American English. The fact that he'd been born—sort of—into the British aristocracy, while Tremayne couldn't shake his Cockney origins and accent no matter how hard he tried, was only one of the reasons Tremayne hated him.

"You think Achmed's scary, wait'll you meet his boss."

"I assume you mean Sheikh Shehabi."

"The old man told you about him, eh? Figured he would."

"He told me about you, too, Alec."

"I was countin' on that. Goin' to the princess' party, are you?"

"I have an invitation."

"So's Sheikh Shehabi." Tremayne pronounced it *shake*, drawing a wince from Achmed that told Chase he spoke English. "Me, too. Movin' up in the world, I am."

"Good for you, Alec. I'll save you a dance on my card."

"Don't bother. You won't be usin' it."

Achmed stepped forward, and Tremayne stepped back. So did Chase, as a dull flicker of lightning backlighted the clouds obliterating the stars.

"This isn't very sporting of you, Alec." Chase retreated another step as Achmed came toward him slowly, stalking him.

"It ain't my idea. It's the sheikh's. He wants your head. Says you owe it to him. That's why he sent Achmed and his sword."

"It's a scimitar, Alec, and Shehabi is a sheikh. If you're gonna walk the walk, better learn to talk the talk."

"Maybe I'll 'ave Achmed cut your tongue out before we take you to the sheikh," Tremayne said, as Chase whirled to run. "Or maybe I'll let Habib do it."

He pronounced it *Habib* rather than *Habeeb*, which drew a glower from the second bearded behemoth in a burnoose, Saville Row suit and flowing robe, who stepped out of the darkness with his blade already drawn. Chase skidded to a halt on the damp cobblestones, fingers clutching the brooch reflexively, his mind searching furiously for a way out.

What he wouldn't give for the pea soup fog that usually rolled in off the bay and swallowed the harbor district by this time of night. Habib made two swift, showy cuts with his scimitar. The whoosh of the blade shot Chase with gooseflesh.

In Tangier he'd watched a demonstration of swordsmanship, had seen blades alarmingly similar to Habib and Achmed's thrown like knives with hair-raising accuracy. He forgot about running and thought about praying, backing up three steps as Habib advanced two.

"Could we have a word first, Alec?"

"What about?"

"Your plan to steal the Phantom. There are a couple of holes in it big enough to drive the royal carriage through."

"Why you offerin' to help me?"

"Professional pride. When I'm dead, you'll be number three on Interpol's most wanted list."

"Hey, that's right, I will," Tremayne said, a fancy-that chuckle in his voice. "No hard feelin's, then?"

"You'd do the same for me."

"Absolutely. Right then, fellas. Hold on a sec."

Habib lowered his scimitar, glared at Tremayne—easily—over the top of Chase's head and said, "Can't you see he's just stalling?" In perfect, upper crust, Oxford-taught English.

"Sod off, Habib," Tremayne snapped, mispronouncing his name again. "The sheikh put me in charge here."

"My name is *Habeeb*," he said, glowering. "And my prince is not a patient man."

"Your prince wants the Phantom, don't he? Nobody knows more about jobs like this than Chase here."

"I'll give you two minutes." Habib bent his left arm, sliding his sleeve past his wrist and a wafer-thin gold Rolex. "And not one second more."

"Righto. Start talkin', old son."

Chase adjusted the sweater tied around his shoulders to hide the parchment sticking out of his pocket, turned to face Tremayne and felt a chill shoot up his back. The fog he'd wished for was beginning to creep silently toward them across the square.

"Besides the two coachmen in the box, there'll be six palace guards disguised as footmen on the carriage," Chase said. *Hurry*, he willed the fog, hoping Habib was still looking at his watch. "How are you going to handle them?"

"Shoot 'em, of course."

"If you shoot the coachmen, who's going to drive the carriage?"

"Me. I been practicin'."

The fog was beginning to thicken and swirl, had already swallowed the pilings of the piers edging one side of the square and the two streets that entered it from the opposite side. Chase had never seen a fog bank roll in so quickly. Not in San Francisco, not even in London.

"Very good, Alec. Planning ahead for a change. Don't forget the postilions. They'll be with the Lipizzaners."

"I'll shoot them, too. All of 'em."

Achmed shook his head and pinched the bridge of his nose, unaware of the fog curling around his ankles.

"If you shoot the horses, Alec, who's going to pull the carriage? Achmed and Habib?"

"I'm not gonna shoot the horses. What kind of a nitwit do you take me for?"

"The Lipizzaners *are* the horses," Achmed growled. "He means the riders on the lead team."

"I know that!" Tremayne rounded on Achmed. "I'm not stupid!"

A wisp of fog spiraled up around his knees. Another engulfed the streetlight, just as the far-off thunder rolled closer and two yellow fog lamps stabbed through the murk from the other side of the square. Achmed whirled, startled, the hem of his robe dissolving in a swirl of mist. So did Chase, unlooping the camera and light meter from around his neck as he tucked and dove for the cobbles, a fraction of a second before Habib's blade sliced through the air where his head had been.

He heard the muffled gun of a car engine as he rolled onto his back, saw headlights stab through the mist and Habib trapped in their beams, looming over him with his scimitar raised for another stroke. With all his strength, Chase swung the Nikon by its strap. It caught Habib under his bearded chin, hard enough to send him staggering backward and knock the blade out of his hand.

Before it clattered onto the stones, Chase had rolled to his feet and spun toward the high beams slicing through the fog toward Tremayne and Achmed at close to fifty miles an hour. They froze for a second like two trapped rabbits, then jumped clear of the chrome grill grinning at them between the beams.

Chase was poised to do the same, until the lights and the nose of the car, a dark blue Mercedes, swung away from him. The brakes squealed, the passenger door sprang open, and the last person on earth Chase expected to see behind the wheel leaned toward him.

"Need a lift?" asked Chief Inspector John Francis, Scotland Yard, retired.

9

OUT OF THE FRYING PAN and into the fire, Chase thought, diving into the car and slamming the door. Francis punched the accelerator and the Mercedes shot away into the fog, tires bumping over the cobblestones.

"It's a sorry world," he said, "when a thief isn't safe on the streets."

"These aren't my streets," Chase replied, breathing deep to get his wind. "Or yours, either."

"I'm afraid they are." Francis glanced at him as he swerved the car into a one-way street leading away from the harbor district. "At least until the princess' coronation."

"Don't worry, Inspector." Chase tucked his camera and light meter under his legs, raised a hand to his chest and felt the proclamation still safely tucked in his pocket. "I'll be long gone by then."

"Or condemned to the dungeons along with Shehabi." Francis eased off the gas as the cobblestones and the fog fell away behind them. "The Grand Duke has no intention of letting either of you leave St. Cristobel with the Phantom."

"What a surprise. Then why did you save my neck?"

"Because I plan to see you, Shehabi, *and* the Grand Duke behind bars before the princess takes the throne. The duke for embezzlement, you for attempted theft and Shehabi for gunrunning."

"Why, you old fox, Inspector. You're no more retired than I am, are you?"

"From the Yard, oh, yes, most definitely. From making sure right triumphs and wrong is punished, never. Not so long as I draw breath."

Which John Francis had been doing for nearly sixty-five years, though he looked no more than fifty. He was a small, neat man with gray hair, silver spectacles and the heart of a lion. He braked at the intersection with Parabello Street and smiled at Chase again as he made a left turn.

"Did you really think I'd work for a man who steals from his own country?"

"Let me guess. That's the reason you took the job."

"More or less. Shehabi's been on Interpol's watch list for years, also under CIA surveillance for selling guns to known terrorists. He's been very careful to stay out of Europe, where most countries have extradition agreements with the United States. Until Savard provided him this golden opportunity to reclaim the Phantom and avenge his family's honor."

Chase made a rueful noise in his throat. "And I thought only Scotland Yard chief inspectors had long memories."

"This is nothing to joke about, Chase. Shehabi intends to kill you. Revenge lives long in the desert."

"In the Highlands, too, Inspector. So who's your real boss?"

"M-5. They're working with the CIA to nail Shehabi. In addition to the Khadafi's pals, he's been supplying arms to the same bunch Savard's been funding. They're using his money and Shehabi's guns to restart nasty little wars the Soviets put a stop to when they dropped the Iron Curtain on them."

"The more things change, the more they stay the same. Why are you telling me all this?"

"So you'll know what you're up against."

Chase had already figured that out—a big wall with no handholds. Francis slowed the Mercedes as they passed the palace, ablaze in a sea of lights atop its soaring hill. Chase wondered what the princess would wear tomorrow night. Something that matched her eyes, he hoped. He wondered, too, if she had any idea what was afoot. Not that it had anything to do with him. None of this had anything to do with him.

"Take my advice and go home, Chase. You don't want to get caught in this kind of crossfire. Shehabi doesn't intend to lose his foothold in St. Cristobel."

"What foothold? He's got the Grand Duke in his pocket, but—"

Chase stopped in midsentence, the rest of what he meant to say shooting a chill up his back. He remembered how easily—and unknowingly—he'd cut the princess off from Diello, the only protection she had.

"But not the princess," Francis finished for him. "Shehabi needs a European base to better service his new clients, and St. Cristobel fits the bill. It's small, politically neutral, and has no real strategic significance."

"So he means to kill the princess and put the Grand Duke on the throne."

"He's next in the line of succession."

"Get Shehabi for gunrunning, my great aunt's fanny," Chase said, an angry edge creeping into his voice. "You're going to nail him for assassinating the princess."

"*Attempted* assassination. The princess is very well protected."

"The hell she is. She's a sitting duck. I've been following her for three days."

"Yes, we know." Francis flipped on the left turn signal and the windshield wipers as they neared Chase's hotel. The wipers cleared the drizzle that had begun to fall with a rubbery squeak that set Chase's teeth on edge. "We let you, since you're not a threat to her safety."

"But I *am* a threat to your setup to bag Shehabi. That's why you want me to be a good little boy and go home."

"Precisely." Francis goosed the Mercedes through a break in traffic, the wipers sweeping again as he braked beneath the portico over the revolving front doors, shut them off and waved the doorman away. "We have Shehabi right where we want him, but if you grab the Phantom he'll abandon his plans for the princess and come after you. We don't want that to happen. We are, in fact, prepared to take steps to make *sure* that doesn't happen."

"Is that a threat, Inspector?"

"It's a promise." Francis bent his left elbow on the steering wheel and turned to look at him. "There's no such thing as a writ of habeas corpus in St. Cristobel. I can have you arrested and detained for as long as I choose, for any reason I choose."

John Francis never bluffed. Chase, on the other hand, rarely told the truth. Not all of it, anyway. He withdrew the proclamation from his shirt, untied the ribbon and handed it over.

"Careful. It's very old and fragile."

Francis turned on the interior light and read the parchment. Three times, holding it close to the windshield and the bright backwash of the hotel's outside security lights. There was a chance he'd cry "Forgery!" and lock him up, but Chase wasn't worried. In addition to being the best damn cop he'd ever run afoul of, the inspector was something of an expert in antiquities. And he was honest—to a fault.

"Amazing," he said, glancing at Chase.

"I came to St. Cristobel to retrieve that parchment."

"And the brooch?"

Chase took it out of his pocket and showed him.

Francis held it up to the windshield and tipped it from side to side. Small as the chips were, they caught the dull outside glow and sent beams of blue-white light flickering across the dash. Where they touched the back of his left hand Chase felt his skin prickle.

"Exquisite." Francis gave him the brooch and bent his elbow on the wheel again. "When do you plan to retire?"

"I haven't thought about it," Chase said, which was true. He never planned any farther ahead than the next job. He slipped the brooch into his pocket and picked up his gear.

"Pity I was never able to nail you."

"Not for lack of trying, Inspector."

"You know Shehabi has an invitation to the ball tomorrow night."

"So do I. I'm attending in Tony's stead. That's the second reason I came to St. Cristobel. I have no reason to steal the Phantom. Not anymore. I've faxed a copy of the parchment home to Glyco. There'll be a suit filed and papers served on the princess when she walks out of the cathedral with the Phantom in her hand."

Francis chuckled. "Cosmo's idea, I'm sure."

"I have a seat booked on British Airways red-eye from San Blanco to Edinburgh tomorrow night." Chase opened the door and swung his legs out of the car. "Feel free to check."

"I will."

Chase swung out of the car, shut the door and stepped onto the curb. The power window slid open behind him as he slung the Nikon and the light meter over his shoulder. Chase turned and saw Francis leaning toward him, elbow bent on the passenger seat.

"Be smart, Chase. Be on that plane tomorrow night."

"I plan to, Inspector."

"For your sake, I hope that's the truth."

The window slid up, and the Mercedes pulled away from the curb. Chase watched until it turned right onto Parabello Street, then he pushed through the revolving doors. For her sake, he hoped the princess planned to wear a flak jacket tomorrow night.

10

THE PRINCESS HAD a plan, all right. A plan that scared even her when she thought about it. So she didn't.

She spent the morning of her birthday being interviewed and photographed by San Blanco's two bilingual newspapers, the *Associated Press* and *Paris Match*. By satellite she appeared on *Good Morning America*.

After lunch, the royal photographer took her birthday portrait. She attended a cabinet meeting, two separate security briefings—one for the ball, one for her coronation—and spent fifteen minutes waving to twenty thousand of her subjects from the balcony overlooking the south courtyard.

A mink coat and a canvas canopy protected her from the chilly April drizzle, yet Molly still felt cold. The rain here was snow in the mountains, beneath a stalled low-pressure cell that had been pumping blustery squalls and petulant thunder over the lowlands since midnight.

Between interviews and photo ops, three stylists retouched her hair and her makeup. Two secretaries followed her everywhere, briefing her on the guest list for the ball. She had only glimpses of her mother, Otto and Danny on the fringe on the chaos, Natalie smiling encouragement, Otto running messages for Danny, who spent most of the day with a cellular phone stuck to his ear.

The first break Molly had came at five-thirty when the guards delivered the Phantom. Today the ritual wasn't a pain in the butt. Today it was a welcome respite. Danny sent Otto in his stead with a note, "Busy cooking goose."

Those three little words did more to ease the pounding headache she'd wakened with than the two Tylenol she'd taken after lunch. Molly sat down with a smile in the red velvet chair and went through the jewel ritual with Captain Maxmillian. Today he was relaxed, almost jovial. Enjoy it while you can, scumbag, Molly thought.

When he gave her the Phantom on its white satin pillow, Molly rose and headed for the vault. Otto held the cushion while she opened the panel and worked the locks. She took the Phantom and he opened the door.

"Wait here for me," she said, knowing he would.

Once she'd slid the scepter and the Phantom onto its shelf, Molly dropped quickly to her heels and peered beneath it. The black nylon barrel tote she'd packed in the middle of the night when she was supposed to be alseep was still safely hidden behind storage boxes bulging with old court documents. She nodded, satisfied, dusted her hands together and left the vault, nodding at Otto.

Danny came in just as Otto shut the door and spun the locks. "See the guards out, would you, Otto?" he asked.

"Certainly." Otto bowed to Molly and herded the guards into the corridor.

"Your uncle's in hock to a sheikh named Shehabi," Danny said, switching on the crystal lamp. "Ring any bells?"

Not only bells, but every alarm Molly had. She sat down, hard, in the red velvet chair as the holograms shimmered to life. "Surely *not* that Shehabi?"

"How many do you know?"

"How much and what for?"

"Dunno how much. The what is to cover the money and the jewels he stole to make loans to every little Tom, Dick and Harry country crawling out from under the Iron Cur-

tain. The clowns stiffed Uncle Dearest, so now he can't repay Shehabi."

"Don't tell me, let me guess." Molly's headache flared
suddenly, sickeningly. "Shehabi wants the Phantom."

"You got it."

"Tell me you have something—*anything*—concrete I can
take to the cabinet for a writ of arrest."

"Not so far. Your uncle's too smart to leave a paper trail.
He holds the reins until the bishop puts your father's crown
on your head, which means you're screwed blue and tat-
tooed."

"Not if I can find a reputable, independent jeweler to appraise the Crown jewels."

"I called every goddamn jeweler in this goddamn country today. Not a single one of them can squeeze you in until
after your coronation."

"My, my, Uncle Karroll, what long fingers you have,"
Molly said, drumming hers on the arm of her chair. "Try
Paris, Danny. Or London. Outer Mongolia, if necessary."

"I'm on it, but it may take a couple days."

Thunder rumbled outside the floor-to-ceiling windows,
rattling the panes and spattering the glass with a fresh gust
of rain. Molly felt another chill ripple through her. What a
difference a day makes, she thought. Yesterday she'd been
dreading her coronation, today she couldn't wait. Neither
could taking steps to protect the Phantom.

"So much for Plan A," she said, pushing to her feet. "Time
for Plan B."

"I don't like Plan B. It stinks. So does letting Sanquist
anywhere near the Phantom. Even to appraise it."

"You don't have to like it." Molly wheeled in her bedroom doorway, her voice sharper than she intended. "You
just have to do it."

"Where are you going?"

"To the bathroom. I haven't been all day."

Molly hurried through the bedroom and locked the dressing room door behind her. The clock on her mirrored table said it was five-forty. Her mother, her maid and the stylists from hell would be here any minute to dress her for the ball.

Thunder rattled the windows and her stomach churned ominously. Molly dashed into the bathroom, hung her head over the toilet but didn't throw up. Her stomach was empty. It was just nerves.

"If you don't like Plan B, Dano," she said, as she rinsed her mouth and washed her hands, "wait'll you see Plan C."

Then she hurried back to the dressing room and unlocked and opened the door. Natalie stood on the other side, her gown for the ball in a bag over her arm, her hand raised to knock.

"Your dinner's here," she said. "Cheeseburger and fries, your favorite. Would you like to eat first?"

Part of Molly wanted to say to hell with the Phantom and St. Cristobel, move to Chicago with her mother and devote her life to stuffing hot dogs in her grandfather's meat packing plant. The rest of her *really* wanted to throw up this time. Instead she said, "Sure," and followed her mother into the living room.

She managed to choke down half a burger, a handful of fries and most of a chocolate milk shake. The food helped her headache, and so did two more Tylenol, but it came back with a vengeance an hour later when Natalie placed the emerald and diamond coronet commissioned for Crown Prince Sandor I's consort on her head.

It weighed nearly three pounds, the matching emerald and diamond necklace almost two. There were pear-shaped emerald earrings to match, two tennis bracelets for each wrist, and a walnut-sized emerald crusted in diamonds for the middle finger of her left hand.

All real, according to Otto. He'd volunteered that his grandfather was a jeweler, had spent half the night in the vault with her and Danny examining the Crown jewels and hatching Plan B. The forgeries were excellent, he'd said, and though he was no expert, he figured nearly a third of the collection were fakes. The one stone he couldn't be sure of was the Phantom.

"A cubic zirconium is a diamond," he'd told her. "Man-made, but a diamond. They will etch glass and are as indestructible as a real stone. I'm sorry, Highness, but to authenticate the Phantom you will need a bona fide expert and a microscope."

Molly hoped a world-class jewel thief would suffice.

"How about your grandfather?" she'd asked.

"Sadly, Highness, my grandfather is dead."

Molly didn't believe him. Or the quiver of anticipation she felt every time she pictured Chase Sanquist in a tuxedo. He was the first interesting man she'd met in months—and he was a thief. An ironic coincidence, since a thief was just was she needed, but a major bummer.

Molly held her mother's arms and stepped into her gown, wiggling into it while Natalie fastened the quarter-carat-each emerald buttons up the back. The dress was floor length with a wrapped bodice and chiffon trains secured to each shoulder by emerald and diamond clips. Molly had paid for it with her own money, most of which she planned to donate to the treasury once she was Crown princess and her uncle no longer controlled her finances.

If there's any money left, she thought, stepping into Italian pumps handmade to match the dress. If Karroll Savard would steal from his own country, why not his own niece?

"You look gorgeous," Natalie said, unzipping her dress bag. "I'll be ready in a minute."

While her mother slipped into the Oleg Cassini she'd seen the day before, a vibrant pink lamé that clung to her still cover-girl-slim figure, Molly stood calmly with her hands folded in front of her. She avoided looking at herself in the mirror, and at the clock ticking on the table. She'd made her decision and her plans. Fidgeting wouldn't change what she had to do—or how.

Subterfuge was an integral part of statecraft. Molly knew that and refused to feel guilty until Natalie swept a brush through her hair, announced she was ready and followed Molly through the bedroom into the living room where Danny was putting on his tuxedo jacket. He stopped and stared at her, blinked twice, then shrugged the coat over his wide shoulders.

"You look like a princess," he said.

"What a coincidence. I *am* a princess."

And a liar, Molly thought, wondering if it showed. Spinning yarns to her uncle was one thing, but she'd never lied to her mother—or Danny. If Otto hadn't knocked and called through the door, giving her the second she needed to swallow the lump swelling in her throat while Danny let him in, she might've blurted out her whole, crazy plan.

"Highness." Otto stepped into the room, decked out in a tux like Danny, and bowed. "The Grand Duke is waiting for you on the mezzanine."

"Thank you, Otto." Molly took a deep breath, squared her shoulders and headed for the doors.

Danny opened them for her and took her arm as they stepped into the hallway. Otto followed with Natalie. It was a short walk to the staircase that swept down to the marble-floored mezzanine on the fourth floor. At the end of another corridor and sweeping staircase lay the third-floor ballroom.

A dozen guards in ceremonial dress waiting below shouldered their pikes when they saw her on the stairs. Karroll Savard turned out of the impatient circle he was pacing on the mezzanine and stopped twisting the signet ring on his finger.

A black and green sash draped from shoulder to hip over his dark blue swallowtail coat glittered with numerous ribbons. His gaze narrowed, sweeping her critically from head to foot as she descended the steps. Molly raised her chin, daring him to find something wrong with her appearance, but he nodded, satisfied, and came forward to take her arm.

A roll of thunder and a strong gust of wind rattled the French doors lining one wall. The draft fluttered the ivory chiffon drapes and shot a chill up Molly's back.

"You look lovely, Marguerite," said the Grand Duke. "How is your ankle?"

"Just fine, Uncle Karroll." Quelling the impulse she felt to slug him, Molly laid her hand on his elbow and smiled. "Ready when you are."

11

READY FOR ANYONE and anything, Molly told herself, so many times she was beginning to believe it. The words ran through her head like a mantra as she stood beside Karroll Savard in the ballroom foyer and guest after guest came down the sweeping pink marble steps to wish her happy birthday.

It was a magnificent staircase, a smaller version of the grand staircase inside the main entrance to the palace, the gallery carpeted in green and black striped runner beneath a mammoth Austrian crystal chandelier. Molly had loved sliding down its gleaming banisters as a child, until she'd broken her left wrist and her father had forbidden it.

The Grand Duke had escorted her here by the south steps from the fourth-floor mezzanine. The guests were entering by the north steps, an army of footmen waiting on the gallery to take wraps and hats and whisk them away.

It was good security, using a side entrance to the palace. The fourth-floor corridor in the three-hundred-year-old north wing led only one place—to this staircase and the ballroom. At the top of the south steps, the ones Molly had come down, there now stood a screen of hammered bronze-and-gold leaf. It weighed several hundred pounds and required a dolly and ten of the pikemen now staggered like a choir on the steps in front of it to wheel it into place.

The scene, stamped in silver on its priceless panels depicting Crown Prince Alisander's victory over Napoléon, when he'd thought to stop by St. Cristobel and sack it on his way home from Russia, gave Molly hope. If her father's namesake could kick Bonaparte's butt, surely she could outfox her uncle, a gunrunning sheikh and a thief with a great tush.

Maybe not with one hand tied behind her back, maybe only by the skin of her teeth, but it was her duty to try, and with any luck her destiny to succeed.

Inspector Francis stood on the gallery to one side of the pikemen, hands folded behind him. He wore a black tuxedo and a red bow tie. He looked perfectly at ease, but his eyes were never still. They swept endlessly around the foyer, the chandelier gleaming on the lenses of his silver spectacles, seeing everything and missing nothing.

He was the only possible fly in the ointment of Plan C. Molly wished she'd paid more attention to the self-composed little detective, that she knew more about him. When his gaze locked with hers over the head of a bowing courtier, Molly started and looked quickly away.

"Le Conte et le Contessa Santella!" the lord chamberlain announced from the gallery. He repeated their names in English as Natalie Savard's former lady-in-waiting came down the steps with her husband.

Molly turned toward them, chancing a glance at the inspector as she offered her hand to be curtsied and bowed over. He gave her a brief, smiling nod, and let his gaze move on. So did Molly, certain that he somehow knew exactly what she was thinking.

"Don't worry," Danny muttered behind her. "The inspector is on Otto's list. He won't let him screw up your plan."

He meant Plan B, of course. Still, Molly shot him a smile over her shoulder, grateful that just this once Danny hadn't a clue what was going on in her head. Then she raised the contessa out of her curtsey and asked about her children, leaning forward to hear her reply as the orchestra began to play inside the ballroom.

A footman thoughtfully closed the set of triple doors closest to the receiving line, but it was too late. Molly already had a bad case of sensory overload. There were simply too many voices and too many faces. None of them the one she wanted, yet dreaded, to see. Her ears felt like somebody had clapped conch shells over them, the contessa's voice hissing like trapped ocean roar inside her head.

Her temples were pounding, made worse by the weight of the coronet. It was padded and not supposed to pinch, but it was rubbing a sore spot over her left ear. It had fit perfectly when she'd tried it on two weeks ago.

The chandeliers stabbed blazing little pinwheels of light in her eyes. Molly caught a glimpse of the ruby lapel watch pinned to the contessa's gown as she moved away with the conte. It was nine-twenty. The steady stream of guests down the staircase had slowed to a trickle, yet there was still no sign of Chase Sanquist.

Molly knew he'd come. Not to dance with her, but to steal the Phantom. She just wished he'd hurry. Outside the foyer windows, thunder rumbled and lightning flickered in the night sky. Molly's headache flared, making her wince. It hurt to smile, hurt to think. She turned her head away from the lights, saw her uncle's face and felt her stomach clutch.

It was white, dead, chalky. His gaze was riveted on the gallery, a sheen of perspiration on his forehead. He looked like he'd seen a ghost.

For an awful half second, as she whipped her head around and saw a white silk robe floating down the staircase, Molly thought she had, too. Her heart started up her throat, until she saw the burnoose wrapped around the tall, dark-bearded man's head, the flash of midnight blue tuxedo in the fluttering front gap of his robe and heard the lord chamberlain's booming announcement, "Sheikh Saddiq el Shehabi!"

His name hadn't been on the guest list, but Molly recognized it. Her breath caught and she felt like Alice, tumbling out of focus down the rabbit hole, as she watched Sheikh Shehabi, the namesake and direct descendant of the sultan from whom Sir Ossric of Glyco had stolen the Phantom, come down the stairs.

Two big men similarly dressed followed him. Bodyguards, obviously. Molly's moment of fright changed to anger, pulse-thumping rage that kept her heart thudding in her throat as she wheeled on her uncle.

"Who in hell do you think you are to invite *him?*" She kept her voice low and the smile on her face, yet still several heads turned in their direction.

"Don't make a scene." The Grand Duke smiled reassuringly at the curious guests. When they moved on, he shot Molly an uneasy sideways glance. "I invited him because I had to, for business reasons, but I never dreamed he'd come."

"What business do you have with a man who supplies guns to terrorists, Uncle Karroll?"

Behind her, Molly heard Danny make an *oh-jeez* noise in his throat, but it was too late to take back her question. She hadn't planned to confront her uncle, but she hadn't planned to see Sheikh Shehabi, either.

The Grand Duke's face paled again, briefly, then flushed a deep, angry red. "That's none of your affair, Marguerite."

"Everything in St. Cristobel is my affair. Present yourself in the audience chamber at nine o'clock sharp Thursday morning. Be prepared to explain your dealings with this man or take up residence in the dungeon."

Her uncle's expression darkened. "Don't threaten me, child."

"I'm not a child," Molly shot back. "I am Princess Royal of St. Cristobel, and *you* are only regent until Wednesday."

Then she spun away from him. The chill that had plagued her since she'd stood waving on the terrace was gone. So was her headache, but the sore spot over her ear was still there.

"This ain't good for Plan B," Danny muttered behind her. "Want me to get rid of these guys?"

"Hell, no," Molly whispered curtly. "The last thing I need is an international incident."

Especially since she planned to create one herself. Unclenching her teeth, Molly put on her best Serene Highness smile and turned to greet the sheikh.

"Your Highness," he murmured, bowing before her.

"Your Highness," she replied, steeling herself as she offered her hand.

She wanted to make a fist out of it and slug him, or at least tuck it behind her, but that would be a terrible insult. It paled next to extortion, but Molly figured she had enough trouble. Or so she thought, until Shehabi reached to take her hand and the lord chamberlain called, "Chastain Sanquist!"

The sheikh's long, brown and perfectly manicured fingers froze. So did Molly's heart. Over Shehabi's bowed head, she saw Inspector Francis unfold his hands and start across the gallery, a grin on his face.

"I don't believe it," Danny muttered.

Molly wanted to look, but couldn't without risking offense to Shehabi. He planted a kiss in midair that came no where near her hand and straightened, his expression unruffled.

"The happiest of birthdays to Your Highness," he said, tucking his hands in the sleeves of his robe. "May I present my kinsmen, Achmed and Habib."

He didn't say which was which. They bowed to her in unison, both well over six feet and two hundred pounds. More than enough to make anybody sweat.

"My uncle, Karroll Savard. Grand Duke and Regent."

"His Grace and I are acquainted." Shehabi accorded her uncle a brief, dismissive nod. "Mr. Sanquist I have looked forward to meeting for a very long time."

He turned toward the staircase, and so did Molly, giving Chase Sanquist his cue to approach. He did so with a smile, the sporran of his kilt swinging as he came down the steps.

"He looks better in a dress than you do," Danny whispered in her ear, a chuckle in his voice.

Magnificent was a better word for the deep, heather-toned blues of his tartan, the perfectly brushed sheen of his darker blue velvet coat and the drape of his plaid. For the brooch securing the plaid to his left shoulder there were only two words—the Phantom.

I was right, Molly thought. *Absolutely, positively right.* The stones were the same color as Chase Sanquist's eyes.

12

THE PRINCESS' EYES looked the same color as the jewels she wore, though Chase could have sworn they weren't that intense a shade of green. They flashed at him like the emeralds clasped around her throat and dangling from her ears, just as deep, just as dark and just as brittle.

She was not overjoyed to see him—or the brooch. He'd considered not wearing it, for about thirty seconds, then he'd taken himself and the parchment back to Jean-Marc's shop. The original would arrive by courier at Glyco within the hour, just in case Cosmo had to spring him from the dungeon. He'd left another copy with Jean-Marc, sent one to the Sanquist family solicitor in Edinburgh and another to Inspector Francis for old times' sake.

He was ready for anything and anyone—except the punch in the gut he felt seeing the princess standing next to Shehabi, most likely oblivious to the fact that he meant to kill her. Chase, too. Before the night was over, if the look on his face was any indication.

It was mostly in his eyes, a pale brown scorch like desert heat, the kind that whipped up sandstorms that flailed a man alive. Shehabi was about his height, Chase figured, the gray threads in his beard hinting at a few more years. Habib stood behind him with Achmed, rubbing his chin and giving Chase a look that promised great unpleasantness. He smiled at him, unfazed. He'd dodged bigger trucks than Habib and lived to tell about it.

The Grand Duke stood on the other side of the princess dabbing his upper lip with a handkerchief. He glared uneasily at Shehabi and affrontedly at Chase. A big fish in a little pond, soon to be eaten by a shark. About two seconds after Chase split with the Phantom.

He'd done enough checking on Shehabi to know he could swallow the Grand Duke whole without belching. He knew, too, that if Inspector Francis hadn't rescued him he'd be dead.

"Good evening, Your Highness." Chase bowed deeply to the princess. "The Earl of Glyco sends his regrets and his best wishes on your birthday."

"Thank you, Mr. Sanquist," said the princess, offering her hand.

Chase cupped his fingers behind hers and pressed them to his lips. He'd done this dozens of times, in dozens of royal houses. He expected the perfection of her manicure, the silky texture of her skin. What surprised him was the tremble in her fingertips and his reaction to it. She had a name, a whole string of them, but he'd never used them, not even when he thought about her. It made it easier to think of her as just the mark, the objective, a thing rather than a living, breathing human being, with nerves and feelings and maybe fears beneath the elegant gown and jewels. Chase wished he didn't know she had a murderer standing beside her. He let go of her hand and straightened.

"May I present my uncle, Karroll Savard, Grand Duke and Regent," she said. "And Sheikh Saddiq el Shehabi."

"Your Grace. Your Highness." Chase bowed to both.

The duke only grunted, exactly what Chase expected from a man stupid enough to fall prey to Shehabi. Court protocol dictated he remain bowing until someone spoke directly to him, which meant the ball was in Shehabi's court. Chase waited, feeling the skin crawl on the exposed back of his neck, trying not to remember that the last time a Sanquist had bowed at court in St. Cristobel he'd had his head handed to him. Literally.

"A pleasure to meet you at last, Mr. Sanquist," Shehabi said. "What a stunning brooch."

Chase straightened, releasing the breath he hadn't realized he'd been holding. "Thank you, Your Highness. A family heirloom."

"Indeed?" Shehabi arched one perfectly shaped and probably waxed eyebrow. "And how did your family come by it?"

"It was a gift from Crown Prince Sandor the First."

The hell it was, said the look the Grand Duke shot Shehabi. He was, Chase noted with satisfaction, sweating again.

"I thought you might be interested, Your Highness, so I brought this along."

He dipped into his sporran, withdrew a copy of the parchment Jean-Marc had made for him that morning and gave it to Shehabi. The part about Chastain Sanquist relinquishing all claims to the Phantom was omitted, otherwise it was an exact copy, a brilliant forgery, of the original. Chase himself had contributed the blood to make the stains.

He watched Shehabi read it, watched the sirocco begin to swirl again in his eyes. On the edge of his peripheral vision, Chase saw the princess lean forward to read the parchment. And smile.

"The original," he said, "is in my cousin the earl's safe at Glyco."

"Of course it is." Shehabi gave the parchment back. "I was given to understand that the Great Eye of Allah has remained intact during all the long centuries since your ancestor took it from my homeland."

He didn't say who'd told him, but he didn't have to. The expression on the Grand Duke's face said it for him. Nor did Shehabi say why it was important, but the murderous look he shot at Savard said it was—very important.

"Le Fantôme was reshaped slightly, Your Highness," the princess put in smoothly, "to fit the royal scepter."

It was the only explanation. Still it was a magnificent, grace-under-fire guess, confirmed by the am-I-right? arch of her eyebrow. The quick wink Chase gave her went unnoticed by the Grand Duke and Shehabi, but not by Diello. He frowned and folded his arms, straining the black satin sleeves of his tux.

"Your Highness. I am keeping you from your guests." Shehabi bowed away from the princess, his gaze riveted on Savard. "And His Grace and I have an important business matter to discuss."

"Of course, Your Highness." The princess smiled at Chase. "Would you escort me, Mr. Sanquist?"

"My pleasure."

He offered his arm, she took it, and he led her away, Diello trailing behind. Glowering, Chase saw, glancing at him over his shoulder as they entered the ballroom.

It was the size of a football field, with pink marble floors and walls. Garlands of roses and orchids wound around the columns supporting the wide mezzanine that ran around three sides. There were baskets of flowers everywhere, green-velvet-covered tables laden with crystal and silver fountains spouting champagne. There were also enough jewels on the two hundred or so guests dancing and talking and laughing around the room to make Chase's mouth water.

At sight of the princess in the doorway, the orchestra playing on the gallery of the branched staircase that led up to the mezzanine fell silent. The lord chamberlain had quit his post in the foyer, and now stood on the princess' left. She nodded to him, and he bowed and faced the room.

"Her Serene Highness," his bass voice boomed solemnly, "Marie-Marguerite Christiana Alistrina Helene Savard, Princess Royal of St. Cristobel."

A jumbled murmur and a flurry of bows and curtsies came from every corner of the room. The princess acknowledged them with a graceful inclination of her chin, raised her arms and both hands to lift her guests to their feet. They rose and the orchestra began to play "Happy Birthday."

Everyone in the room sang. So did Chase, suppressing a smile at the memory of the regal creature beside him swinging along Parabello Street in her jeans and her boots and her Bears cap. Which person, he wondered, was the real one?

The song ended, the guests applauded, and the princess smiled and waved. The orchestra leader raised his baton, a waltz began, and the dancing resumed.

"Would you like to dance, Your Highness?" Chase asked.

"Yes, thank you."

He led her down from the raised dais edging the dance floor, took her in his arms and moved her into the steps of a Strauss waltz. Her right hand fit small and cool in his, and the chiffon of her gown felt soft as silk against his left palm. Up close her emeralds were exquisite, the settings alone and the gold in her coronet worth a bloody fortune.

The princess titled her chin up to look at him, an amused glimmer in her eyes. "You're drooling, Mr. Sanquist."

"Forgive me, Highness. I've never danced with a princess before."

"I had no idea this piece existed." She lifted her left hand from his shoulder and touched the brooch, her head tipped curiously to one side. "Obviously, neither did my uncle. How *did* you get your hands on it?"

"You saw the parchment, Highness."

"Yes, I saw it, but I don't believe a word of it."

"Are you calling me a liar?"

"No, Mr. Sanquist. I'm calling you a thief."

He pulled her closer and smiled. "I'd rather you call me Chase."

The stroke of his fingertips on the small of her back made Molly shiver. It was nothing personal, merely an involuntary reaction, her body adjusting from the drafty foyer to the overwarm ballroom.

"You needn't be so obvious," she replied, easing away from him. "I have every intention of inviting you to my apartment."

That surprised him, and excited him. His eyelashes were very thick, and several shades darker than his hair. They made a tiny, upward leap, then swept down. A chandelier whirled by overhead, spinning beams of light from its crystal facets. On his shoulder the brooch flashed a deep, sultry sapphire. So did his eyes beneath half-lowered lids.

"How do we give Diello the slip?" he asked.

He wouldn't believe me even if I told him, Molly thought. Besides, he meant something else entirely, a something else that sent another shiver sliding up her spine.

"It's all arranged." She glanced away from him, nodding as they neared the far end of the ballroom. "Meet me here, behind the middle pillar beneath the mezzanine, at ten forty-five."

Chase looked where she nodded. The pillars were marble like everything else in the ballroom, wound with garlands of pink rosebuds and white orchids, and thick enough to hide ten pikemen.

"The middle pillar?" he asked.

"Yes."

"You mean this one right here?" He nodded at the pillar as he waltzed her closer to it.

"Yes. This one."

"You're sure it isn't a column? It looks more like a column to me than a pillar."

"I don't care what you call it. Just meet me behind it at ten forty-five."

One second they were dancing, the next Molly was spinning in a dizzy circle. A startled yelp escaped her as Chase Sanquist whirled her off the dance floor into the deep shadows beneath the mezzanine.

She felt petals crush beneath her shoulders as he pressed her up against the pillar, and a twinge in the sore spot beneath her coronet. When he spread his hands above her shoulders, she caught her breath and tasted roses on her tongue.

"You mean like this?" he asked.

Molly laughed, light-headed from the spin and Chase Sanquist's nearness. He was taller and heavier than he'd looked in the café. His shoulders were broader, too, but there was no padding in his jacket, only muscle in the velvet-clad arms pinning her to the pillar. Or the column, or the post, or whatever he'd called it.

"Only if you insist," she said.

"I insist," he said, and kissed her.

He hadn't meant to. He'd only meant to make her laugh and keep her off balance. A mark who was never sure what was coming next was easier to mold to his purpose. So was her mouth, shaping itself to his as he slid his right arm around her and pulled her closer. He hadn't meant to do that, either.

Any more than Molly meant to put her arms around his neck, but that's where they were when he lifted his head and she opened her eyes. He looked as surprised as she felt, his eyebrows slightly raised, a pulse beating in his temple.

"I insist," she said shakily, "that you let me go."

"So do I," Diello growled from the other side of the pillar.

13

THE LOOK on Diello's face made Chase wish one of them was on the other side of the moon. Preferably Diello. He'd folded his arms across his chest again, straining his sleeves over his thirty-eight-inch-at-least biceps.

"This is a dry run for Plan B, Danny," the princess told him calmly. "Just in case somebody catches us back here."

"Oh." Diello's features relaxed out of their which-leg-would-you-like-me-to-break glower, and Chase's heart slid out of his throat. "Got a watch, Sanquist?"

Chase stepped away from the princess and pushed his lace-trimmed cuff off his wrist. "Are we going to synchronize?"

"In your dreams." Diello looked at his watch. "It's ten-seventeen. Be back here in twenty-eight minutes."

"I wouldn't miss it," Chase said, plucking rose petals out of the princess' hair.

The brush of his knuckles against her cheek made Molly's stomach flutter. The smile he gave her made her wish she was the attraction rather than the Phantom.

"What's Plan B?" he asked.

"You'll find out in twenty-eight minutes."

"Twenty-seven," Diello said.

"Twenty-seven, then," she corrected, worrying a finger under her coronet as she slipped away into the crowd with Diello behind her.

Chase kept to the shadows until he reached the next pillar, then stepped around it and leaned his shoulder against it. The princess was making her way around the ballroom greeting her guests. Neither she nor Diello looked back at him. Very smart. They at least had some idea what they were doing, which was more than he could say for himself.

He had no idea why he'd kissed her. Maybe he'd been overcome by the emeralds. He'd always been a sucker for them. It was an understandable attraction, when he thought about it. Who better to keep a jewel thief in jewels than a princess with a palace full?

The Grand Duke came into the ballroom and paused on the dais to refold his handkerchief in his pocket. He looked drained and distraught—nibbled rather than gnawed—even from across the dance floor. Chase watched him work his way smiling and nodding, into the room, saw Shehabi materialize in the doorway sans Achmed and Habib.

The sheikh hovered for a moment like a wraith, then melted into the crowd following the same path as Savard. Chase wondered where Achmed and Habib were, and frowned when it dawned on him he hadn't seen Alec Tremayne.

An alarming coincidence to a man who didn't believe in them. Scanning the crowd for any sign of the princess or Inspector Francis, Chase pushed off the pillar. He had a bad feeling, confirmed by the old familiar chill up the back of his neck, that Plan B—whatever the hell it was—couldn't wait twenty minutes.

He saw a flash of green to his right and started toward it, heard a wolf whistle behind him and glanced over his shoulder at Natalie Savard coming toward him with two glasses of champagne. Her pink lamé gown was a knockout. So was her figure. Chase wondered if her daughter had inherited all of her curves. He knew firsthand she'd been gifted with at least a couple.

Despite the urgency he felt, Chase stopped and said to her, "You're the first whistle I've had tonight."

"But not the last. You've got better legs than I do."

Chase laughed, took the glass she offered and put a kiss on her cheek.

"I saw you collected your dance from my kid."

"Some kid." Chase smiled. "Some dancer."

Natalie arched a knowing eyebrow. "Some kisser?"

"And then some."

"In my day, we did that sort of thing behind potted plants. Cosmo kissed me once behind a Ficus benjamina."

"That silver-haired old devil."

"I think the attraction was my sapphire necklace."

"Runs in the family."

"Molly knows all about you, Chase. Francis told her."

"He's only doing his job, Natalie."

"When are you going to do yours?"

"In about twenty minutes."

"Then here's to success," she said, raising her glass.

"You aren't going to scream for the guards?"

"Hell, no. My dear, darling *ex*-brother-in-law will be blamed for the theft. He'll be completely discredited, and Molly will be able to rule on her own without his interference."

"I'll drink to that." Chase touched his glass to hers and did.

He was thirsty, and startled when he looked over the top of Natalie's head and saw Shehabi, who hadn't been there a second ago. He stood smiling about five feet away with his hands—and God only knew what else—tucked up his sleeves.

"There's a man standing behind you wearing a sheet." Chase pressed his empty glass into Natalie's hand. "Keep him busy for about five minutes and I'll owe you a mambo."

"Make it two and you got a deal."

"Two it is." Chase put a kiss on her brow and melted into the throng of dancers, hoping he'd live to deliver.

He felt like somebody had slipped an ice cube down his back and set fire to his left shoulder. He'd been aware of the brooch perched there since he'd pinned it to his plaid. It had taken him twenty minutes in front of the mirror in his hotel room to get it just right, had found himself distracted more than once by the dazzle of the stones in the glass.

It took him a good three minutes to find the princess, which only left him two to duck Shehabi. She stood with Diello talking to Inspector Francis. What luck.

What's up? Molly wondered, catching a glimpse of Chase out of the corner of her eye. A half a second later, she wondered what in hell he was *thinking*, walking toward them with his I'm-just-a-wealthy-ne'er-do-well smile on his face.

"Your Highness." He gave her a half bow, then turned to Francis. "Good evening, Inspector."

"Evening, Chase. Pleasure to see you."

Molly held her breath, half expecting Inspector Francis to slap a handcuff on Chase's wrist. Instead, they simply shook hands. What was this?

"I haven't seen Alec yet this evening, have you?"

"Tremayne? *Here?* You're joking."

"Not unless he was when he told me he had an invitation. Sheikh Shehabi's two kinsmen have gone missing, as well."

"Uh-oh," Danny murmured in Molly's ear.

"That hardly seems coincidental," Inspector Francis said thoughtfully.

The frown that crossed his face confirmed Molly's suspicion that something was definitely up. "Inspector," she began, but he held up one hand to her as he raised the other to the tiny transmitter in his ear.

He bowed his head, listening, then jerked up his chin so suddenly Molly jumped, a chill of alarm shooting through her.

"The palace switchboard has just received a bomb threat," he said curtly to Diello. "Get the princess out of here. I'll find the Grand Duke and start evacuating the guests."

Molly's heart seized. So did her breath in her throat.

"This isn't Plan B, is it?" Chase asked Danny.

"Of course it isn't. It's probably just a crank."

"Maybe."

Neither Danny nor Chase Sanquist sounded convinced.

Neither was Molly. She whirled and gripped Danny's arms. "Find my mother and get her out of the palace."

"She hired me to protect you," he growled.

"Don't gimme any lip, Diello." Molly made a fist and smacked him in the chest, hard enough to make him grunt and her knuckles pop. "Just do it."

"Okay, okay." He caught her wrist as she wound up to belt him him again. "Take Sanquist with you and get outta here."

He wheeled away and ducked into the crowd. The princess grabbed Chase's arm and bolted for the door.

"Not so fast." He dragged her beside him, tucked her hand around his elbow and held it there. "You'll start a panic."

"Sorry," Molly said. Stay calm, breathe deep and *think*, she told herself. "Who's Alec Tremayne?"

"A thief and a nasty little thug. The kind you want out in the open where you can keep an eye on him."

Lightning flashed bright as daylight outside the French doors at the far end of the foyer as they passed through the ballroom doors. A monstrous roll of thunder crashed over the palace, reverberating off the walls and all the way up Molly's spine as she saw the empty staircase ahead of them.

"Where are the pikemen?" she asked warily.

"Probably looking for the bomb," Chase replied, hustling her across the foyer and up the steps. "Hoax or not, they have to check."

On the gallery, she turned left and he cut to the right. With their arms linked, neither of them went anywhere. The chandelier flickered overhead, and cool, damp air washed a chill through Molly as she looked at Chase over her shoulder.

"The closest exit is this way," he said.

"I'm not leaving here without the Phantom," she told him bluntly, "and no one else is leaving *with* it. Including you, Mr. Sanquist."

Chase could almost hear the ring of chain mail on the marble floor. The gauntlet was thrown. He smiled, his senses and his heartbeat quickening.

"How about if we leave with it together?" he suggested, abandoning his plan to deliver the princess to safety and come back for the Phantom under the pretext of helping to evacuate the guests. He'd find another way to ditch her.

"Exactly what I had in mind, Mr. Sanquist. This way."

She led him up the south steps and helped him move the screen. Edging just the single end panel far enough out of the way so they could squeeze past it took every ounce of their combined strengths. Once on the other side, the princess kicked off her high heels, picked them up and ran down the corridor toward the south wing.

The wall lights flickered and thunder echoed faintly behind them. The princess was barely winded when they reached the end of the hallway. Chase made a note of that, and of the cautious way she peered around the intersecting wall before leading him across a marble-floored mezzanine glistening with puddles of rain that had blown in under the French doors.

He followed her up the short, curved flight of stairs to the fifth floor of the south wing, his heart racing and his ears ringing. He couldn't account for it, or the dizziness that overcame him halfway up the steps. He put one hand on the wall, felt the chill in his skin and shook his head.

The ringing in his ears subsided to a fuzzy murmur like voices whispering very far away. It was eerie and unnerving as hell, but he fought it down with a deep breath and concentrated on climbing the stairs without falling on his face.

He managed it, barely, keeping his hand on the wall and gritting his teeth as the princess led him to her apartment. When she opened the double doors the murmur swelled to a roar in his head that nearly staggered him. He wondered if Natalie had been feeding him a line of bull about the Grand Duke, if she'd slipped him something in the champagne.

He saw double of the walls in the princess' living room. Transparent walls shimmering where none should be. His equilibrium failed, nausea churned, and spots began to dance before his eyes. He blinked to clear them and saw the princess waving him urgently inside. She looked like Shiva, the Hindu god with four arms undulating around her head.

"Hurry up, hurry up, hurry up," she said, her voice echoing in his head like a yodel in the mountains.

Chase took a deep breath, careful aim at the floor and a woefully misjudged step that sent him falling into the room. He flung out his arms to grab the back of a sofa that dissolved in his grasp, staggered sideways and braced himself to crash into the wall dead ahead.

"Stop!" the princess cried. "You'll set off the alarm!"

Her scream cut through the roar and the drunken fog in his head. Rational thought and his equilibrium came back, about a half a second too late to keep him from lurching headfirst through the hologram field.

14

IT WAS IMPOSSIBLE, but the alarms didn't scream, and the guards who should have come boiling through the doors didn't.

I'm dead, Molly thought, as she stood just inside the door with her hands over her eyes. There really was a bomb and it went off. I didn't feel it or hear it, but it did, and now I'm dead. Or in the Twilight Zone.

"Holy shit."

Molly lowered her hands and saw Chase standing half in and half out of the fireplace-wall hologram. He looked as stunned and dazed as she felt. She swallowed, hard, then clapped a hand over her mouth as he stepped out of the beam.

Nothing happened. He stepped into it again, and still nothing happened.

"What in the name of all that's holy is going on?" Molly asked shakily.

"How in hell would I know?" Chase snapped. "How in hell do I turn it off?"

"Flip the switch on the crystal lamp twice."

He did, with an unsteady hand. The first click deactivated the field, returning the room to its original proportions, the second turned on the lamp. It flickered in a blazing flash of lightning, then went out. So did every other light in the apartment and the hallway behind Molly in a horrendous boom of thunder that vibrated the windows.

"There's your answer." Chase laughed in the darkness, his voice shaky with relief. "The storm must've shorted the system. Or the main transformer got hit by lightning. How long does it take the backup to come on line?"

"Thirty seconds. How do you know so much about my palace, Mr. Sanquist?"

"I know a lot about a lot of things, Your Highness."

The lights came on just as Molly mentally counted twenty-eight. Chase still stood by the crystal lamp, but now a small, slight man in a leather jacket and pants as black as his slicked-back hair leaned against the fireplace.

His arms were folded and he held a gun, a big, chrome-plated gun, in his left hand. Molly had never seen him before, but she had a sinking feeling she knew who he was.

"'Allo, Chase," he said. "Nice of you to bring the princess by to open the vault so's I don't have to blow it up."

Like he'd just blown up Plan C—but maybe not. If she was careful, Molly thought, watching Chase turn toward the fireplace, if she did what was expected and wasn't too obvious about it, maybe she could still pull it off.

"Hello, Alec," Chase said, confirming the oily little thug's identity. "I had a feeling you might be here."

"That's *why* I'm here, 'cause I knew *you* would be," Tremayne said smugly. "Outfoxed the fox at last, I have."

He threw back his head and laughed. Molly saw her chance to do the expected and whirled for the door. She didn't expect to see one of Sheikh Shehabi's kinsmen looming behind her with a curved sword in one hand, and let out a startled yelp.

"Good one, Habib," Tremayne said, and laughed harder.

"Ha*beeb*," the huge man growled over Molly's head, then bowed to her and said, "Please step inside, Highness."

Molly did, wishing she hadn't thrown her shoes God knew where when she'd clapped her hands over her eyes. She was shivering, from rage and fright as much as cold.

"Right, then, Princess." Tremayne motioned to her as Habib closed the doors. "Over here and pop the locks like a good little highness."

"Why? So you can kill me quicker? Rot in hell."

No one had to tell her that was the plan. She'd figured it out when she'd seen the gun. Everything was clear to her now, her uncle's nervousness, Shehabi's presence at the ball, even the bomb threat. It was a diversion to sidetrack Inspector Francis and the guards while Tremayne stole the Phantom.

"Who said I was going to kill you?" Tremayne asked.

"Since when are guns and swords safecracking tools?"

"Don't get hoity-toity with me, Highness. I've got lots of lovely dynamite over here, and I'd just as soon blow your pretty little head off as the vault door."

It was an idle threat, and Molly knew it. An explosion would attract attention and more guards than his gun and Habib's sword could handle.

"You'll find matches on the mantel to light the fuses."

Crown Prince Sandor would be proud, Chase thought. God knew he was. She was cool as ice under fire, and in danger of getting her pretty little head blown off if she pushed Tremayne much further.

"Hold on, Alec," Chase said. "Let's compromise."

"Sod you. I don't do that kinda thing. Not with blokes."

Chase heard Habib make a weary, Allah-give-me-strength noise in his throat and prayed along with him, prayed to God Shehabi hadn't sent Tremayne to steal the Phantom and Habib to kill him and the princess. But he knew he had, and he knew who'd sent the bomb threat.

"Look, Alec," he went on, hoping the princess had sense enough to play along. "Her Highness is as rich as Croesus. She doesn't care a fig about the Phantom. She was going to give it to me, as a matter of fact. I'll give it to you, how's that? Then you and Habib can be on your way."

It was the wrong approach. Chase saw it in Tremayne's narrowed eyes and the ugly snarl that curled one side of his mouth. He pushed off the mantel and leveled the gun at the bridge of Chase's nose.

"I'm sick of you treatin' me like I'm stupid. No bleedin' way is she gonna *give* anybody the Phantom."

"Why shouldn't I? It's mine, and I've already got more diamonds than I know what to do with," Molly put in quickly, her heart pounding at the sight of the gun pointed at Chase. "I'm so tired of everyone squabbling over the Phantom I could scream. I'll be glad to see the last of it."

Tremayne looked like he could kiss her. Chase swore if they got out of this alive he would.

"You aren't puttin' me on, are you?" Alec asked warily.

"Of course she is, you fool." Habib strode forward with his sword half raised. "Get on with it. My prince is—"

"Back off." Tremayne swung the gun toward Habib so quickly Molly caught her breath as the muzzle flashed past her. "I've got your number, Habib. You mean to lop off my head once you've got the Phantom, but I ain't gonna let that happen. You raise that sword another half inch and I'll drop you like a big, fat rock."

"You waste precious time arguing," Habib said, lowering his sword. "We are already behind schedule."

"I'll waste all the bloody time I please. Throw the sword over here."

Habib raised his scimitar and hesitated. Chase thought he meant to hurl it at Alec's chest, but instead he gave it a gentle toss. It plopped harmlessly onto the carpet in front of Alec, who nudged it aside with his toe.

"Right then, Highness. Prove you mean what you say and open the vault."

"First tell me there's no bomb," Molly said. "Tell me my guests will be safe." And my mother and Danny and Otto, she prayed.

"Course there's a bomb. Wouldn't be much of a threat without a bomb, would it? It ain't goin' off, though. It ain't got a detonator."

Chase was sure Alec was telling the truth so far as he knew it, but the quick glance Habib stole at his Rolex and the visible swallow he made told Chase something else. It told him the bomb *did* have a detonator—and it told him it was ticking.

"I'll need Mr. Sanquist's help," the princess said. "The vault door is very heavy."

"Give Her Highness a hand, Chase, while I keep an eye on Habib here."

"Ha*beeb*," the big man said through gritted teeth.

He looked like he wanted to kill Alec. Chase hoped he'd get the chance, and followed the princess to the fireplace. Her fingers trembled as she pressed the navel of a gold-leaf cherub plucking a harp on the mantel facing. A baroque cupboard built into the rococo wall on the right-hand side of the fireplace slid aside and there was the vault, its steel door and four locks gleaming in the lamplight.

The storm unleashed another barrage as she worked the combinations. Thunder crashed, rain pelted the windows, and the lights flickered again. Over the murmur in his head, Chase heard the howl in the wind and felt ice slide down his back. If he was as crazy and vengeful as Shehabi, where would he plant a bomb?

A vicious bolt of lightning exploded outside the windows, near enough that Chase felt his wool plaid crackle and the princess almost jump out of her dress. The lights sputtered, and her fingers leapt off the third lock, spinning the dial and the tumblers out of sequence.

"Steady," Chase whispered, cupping her shoulders in his hands. "I'm not going to let them kill us."

"What are you going to do?"

"I wish to God I knew."

"No talkin'!" Tremayne barked, his voice edgy. "Just get the bleedin' door open!"

The princess shot him a glare and started on the third lock again. Chase glanced at Alec, saw the tension etched in his tightly drawn features, and dropped his gaze to the scimitar gleaming on the carpet in the glow of the crystal lamp. It lay roughly in the middle of the room, maybe an inch or two closer to him. It wasn't much of an advantage but he'd take it. With Alec already straining the limits of his intellect, it might be enough—if he had the guts to use it.

The princess gave the fourth lock a final turn and grasped the thick handle with both hands. She pushed it down as far as she could, breaking the seal with a faint hiss.

The murmur in Chase's head climbed a decibel or two as she stepped back and gestured him toward the door. He changed places reluctantly, still trying to think of a way to keep them alive and avoid giving the Phantom to Tremayne.

He pushed the handle two notches lower than the princess had been able to and pulled. The door budged maybe an inch. He dug his feet into the carpet, leaned back and threw his shoulders as well as his arms into it. The door moved maybe four more inches.

"How much does this damn thing weigh?"

"I don't know," the princess replied, puzzled. "I can barely move it, but it usually comes right open for Danny."

"If I didn't know better—" Chase threw his head back, teeth gritted, and levered all his strength against the door "—I'd say there was somebody pulling from the other side."

"Stop muckin' around and open the bloody door!" Alec shouted furiously.

"C'mon, baby." Chase give a mighty pull and wished he had Diello's thirty-eight-inch biceps. "Come to Papa."

The door flew open, pinning Chase against the fireplace and cracking his head against the mantel. He saw stars and heard every church bell in St. Cristobel ringing in his ears.

The princess pulled the door off him. It swung smoothly back on its hinges and hung half-open, a wedge of light cast by the fluorescent tubes that came on automatically spilling out of the vault.

"Are you all right?" the princess asked, her voice sounding tinny inside his head.

"I think so." Chase pushed himself off the mantel and shook his throbbing head. "Yeah."

"Quit stalling!" Alec shouted, red-faced. "Bring me the Phantom *now!* Before I blow your goddamn heads off!"

"Get it yourself!" Molly spun on him furiously, her heart pounding in her throat. It was risky, but it was exactly what he'd expect her to do.

"Just for that, your hoity-toity highness," Tremayne jeered at her, "you can bring me the whole royal scepter."

"The hell I—"

"Right away, Alec." Chase grabbed her arm and towed her into the vault.

Molly let herself be dragged, then wrenched away from him. With both hands, she grabbed the inside handle and pulled, the weight of the door wrenching the muscles she'd strained opening it herself at four in the morning.

"Help me!" she whispered tersely to Chase.

He either didn't or couldn't hear her. He stood staring blank-eyed and slack-jawed at the Phantom.

"God damn it!" Tremayne howled frantically on the other side of the door. "Stop them, Habib!"

Chase heard him and whirled, shaking his head to clear the blue-white lights dancing in front of him. His eyes focused on the princess and the door swinging slowly inward.

"Are you crazy?" He leapt at her and tried to wrest the handle away from her. "I can steal it back before Alec gets to the front door."

"Trust me," she panted, gasping with effort. "I know another way out."

Chase had no reason to trust her, but every reason to distrust Alec Tremayne. He stopped pushing and started pulling just as Habib caught the handle from the other side, bellowing at Allah in Arabic and tugging the door toward him.

"No!" the princess screamed, swearing and pulling.

Wishing he'd had Diello's biceps again, Chase gave a mighty heave and the door crashed shut, enveloping them in darkness. He shoved the handle up as far as it would go and held it, heard the princess spin the locks over her ragged, frantic breathing.

"That's it," she said shakily. "We're locked in."

"Are you sure?"

"Positive. I've locked this vault a thousand times."

Chase let go of the handle and sagged against the door. He heard the princess sigh and her gown rustle as she collapsed against the door beside him.

"We're safe now," she said, half a second before the bomb exploded.

15

THE CONCUSSION knocked Chase to his knees. He heard the princess cry out, groped for her in the dark and clutched a handful of her gown. He dragged her against him and wrapped his arms around her. Something hard and sharp whacked him under the chin, but he barely felt it. The princess clung to him, shivering, the shelves tearing loose from the walls and raining jewels on their heads.

When the roar died away, Chase cautiously lifted his head. He couldn't hear much except a faint crackle beyond the vault door and the incessant murmur inside his head. He couldn't see. He closed his eyes and wished he could, then opened them and realized with a start that he could. Not well, but he could see, the edges of his vision smeary and tinged a faint blue.

The vault was a total wreck. Chunks of the ceiling and all but the top two shelves had fallen. There were jewels scattered everywhere, twinkling dully beneath a film of dust.

"Are you okay?" Holding the princess by her elbows, Chase rocked back on his heels.

She blinked at him dazedly, the royal scepter clutched in her arms. The Phantom flashed a brilliant, dizzying blue, untouched by the dust coating everything else. Chase didn't know whether to laugh or cry.

"I think so." She reached up and yanked off the coronet the explosion had knocked half off her head, winced and rubbed her scalp above her left ear. "Damn crown. It's been pinching my head all night."

"You lost an earring," Chase told her.

Her elaborately upswept hair was powdered with dust and hung mostly in her face. She shoved it out of her eyes and blinked in his general direction. "Can you see?"

"Sort of."

"Good. Hold this and help me up."

Chase tucked the scepter under one arm and eased her to her feet. She wobbled unsteadily, then pulled away from him.

"I'm perfectly *fine*." She shoved her hair out of her face again with a shaky hand. "I'm sure Shehabi and my *dear* uncle will think I'm dead, but that's okay. Let them enjoy it until I get out of here. Then I'll make them wish *they* were dead."

Perfectly fine, hell. She was perfectly livid, nearly hyperventilating, sucking air like a jet engine, angry enough not to realize that if Shehabi and her uncle thought she was dead, Natalie and Diello would, too.

"Save your snit until we're out of here, Highness. Then you'll have plenty of oxygen to rant and rave."

"Go to hell, Sanquist!" She spun toward him, stubbing her bare toes against a broken shelf, blind in the pitch blackness that was blue-tinged murk to Chase. He caught her elbow and kept her from falling, felt her shiver and watched her hold a deep breath for a six count.

"I'm sorry," she said, letting the breath go. "I've never had anyone try to kill me before."

"Quite all right, Princess. Neither have I."

"How can you see?" She raised a hand to her face, wiggled her fingers, but didn't blink. "I'm blind as a bat."

"I eat lots of carrots," Chase said, and let it go at that. He had no idea why he could see. Nor did he want to think about it. Not now, anyway.

"There is—at least there *was*—a black nylon bag with a couple flashlights in it under the bottom shelf on this wall." The princess pointed toward the back corner. "If you'll get it for me, I can get us out of here."

Chase found the bag wedged between two taped-up cardboard boxes, shoved them aside with a pile of rubble and carried the bag to the princess. She draped it over her shoulder by its webbed strap, unzipped it and fished out two flashlights. She gave Chase one, switched the other on, tucked it under her arm and pulled out a pair of black high-top Reeboks.

Then she held out her hand to him. "I'll take the scepter, please."

He gave it to her, amused that she thought squirreling it away in a black nylon tote would keep it safe. When she leaned against the wall to put on and lace her shoes, Chase turned his flashlight on so she could see.

"Is this Plan B?" he asked, wondering what else she had in the bag.

"No, Mr. Sanquist, it's Plan C." She straightened off the wall and played the beam of her flashlight around the vault. "My God, what a mess. How big a bomb do you think it was to wreck this kind of havoc behind six feet of steel?"

"Plenty damn big," Chase said curtly. The crackle he knew meant fire outside the vault was growing louder, which meant the flames were getting closer. The way his luck was running, the sprinkler system would come on and drown them. "I know I'm going to be sorry I asked, but—what's Plan C?"

"Your only ticket out of here, Mr. Sanquist." She quit flashing the light around and turned to face him. "My uncle has been stealing stones from the Crown jewels for some time and replacing them with fakes. Since Shehabi showed up tonight to claim the Phantom, I'm no longer worried that it's been switched. My primary concern is getting it safely out of St. Cristobel until my coronation, whereupon I can toss my uncle in the dungeon for treason. Since you wouldn't take the job even if I were willing to hire you—"

"Don't tell me," Chase cut in. "And since you know the way out of here and I don't, either I agree to take you and the Phantom with me or we sit here and die of asphyxiation."

"Precisely." The princess smiled.

"Well, there's a tough choice. I agree. Now get us the hell out of here."

"Hold this." She passed him the bag without looking at him, turned her back on him and pointed her flashlight beam on the boxes he'd just moved. "Push one of those over here."

Chase shoved the closest box toward her. She lifted her skirt and climbed on top of it, pointing her flashlight at one of the shelf supports shaped like an inverted hook.

"Hold the light here," she said.

Chase took the flashlight and did. She stood on her toes and jumped to reach the support, wrapped both hands around it and pulled. Nothing happened. She tried again, grasping the hook and swinging off the box to throw her whole body weight into it. This time, Chase heard a low rumble, felt the floor quiver and saw the middle section of vault wall begin to slide open. A whoosh of musty but breathable air whooshed through the slowly widening gap.

"Told you." The princess grinned at him, swinging from the brace like a kid on a jungle gym, her hair drooping in her face again.

He laughed and stepped toward her, looping his arm around her waist. Molly put her hands on his shoulders, thinking he meant to help her down. Instead he kissed her, quick and hard. So hard she thought she could hear their teeth grinding together, until he turned his head and she saw the passageway starting to close.

He dropped her and flung himself into the opening, putting his back against the panel and thrusting one leg against the wall. Molly grabbed her bag and started digging through the wreckage on the floor.

"What are you doing?" he asked, grunting and pushing.

"Salvaging what I can of my heritage, not to mention my country's wealth, from my lying, cheating, thieving uncle." Molly shoved the emerald coronet and a tangle of necklaces into the bag and dug into another pile of debris. "Just hold the door a minute."

"You hold the door," he growled, just barely, over the groan of the panel. "At least I know the difference between blue topaz and sapphires."

Molly whipped her head toward him, clutching a handful of twisted platinum and blue stones. "These are *fakes?*"

"Probably," he gritted between clenched teeth. "It's hard to tell for sure while I'm being crushed."

Molly shoved them in the tote anyway and uncovered another heap of stones. The panel and Sanquist both groaned louder. Her heart racing with the need to hurry, Molly dug deeper and found another pile of tangled jewelry, shoved it in the bag and zipped it as she whirled to her feet and grabbed her flashlight.

Sanquist had tucked his flashlight under his chin and flung both arms against the wall. Molly tugged it free as she sidled past him, then backed out of the way as he slid out of the opening behind her. The panel thudded home with a dull, echoing boom that raised gooseflesh on her arms.

"Where does this go?" Sanquist asked, breathing hard and taking his flashlight.

"The dungeon." Molly raked her hair out of her face again and wished she had a rubber band. "The vault used to be Prince Sandor's dressing room. He used to sneak out after his wife was asleep to watch prisoners being tortured."

And to help, I'll bet, Chase thought, shining the beam down the narrow, low-ceilinged passageway. "Charming family you come from," he said.

"I could say the same about you."

"Later. Once we're out of here, we can have a rousing game of family feud." He took her elbow and led her forward, shining the beam on the stone floor. "Does anybody else know about this passage?"

"No," she said, but there was a second's hesitation in her voice. "I don't think so," Molly amended, when Sanquist stopped and scowled at her. "My father showed it to me before he died. He said Uncle Karroll didn't know about it."

The Grand Duke was one thing, Shehabi was something else.

"I don't suppose," Chase asked, "you have a gun in your little black bag?"

"Me?" She arched an eyebrow. "Don't you have one?"

"No. I don't like guns." Chase took her arm and started down the passage again. "They scare me almost as much as the people who use them."

He was rapidly developing an aversion to swords, too, but didn't say so. He didn't like rats, either, and kept a lookout for furry, four-legged vermin. He was sure he'd seen the last of the two-legged variety—for a while, anyway—until Achmed materialized from the shadows a couple yards ahead of them, where the passage bottomed out and turned to the left.

There was damp seeping out of the stones underfoot now, and a dull light gleaming beyond the curved wall. It was just enough to show the gold tooth in Achmed's mouth as he smiled and drew his scimitar from the folds of his robe.

The princess sucked in a sharp breath beside Chase and dug her nails into his arm. "So much for nobody else knows about this passage," he muttered to her.

"My prince knows many things, Mr. Sanquist," Achmed said. "Once the Great Eye of Allah and the brooch you wear are returned to him and made one again, he will know all that there is to know of all things under heaven."

"If your prince knows so much," Chase replied, vowing to buy a gun first chance he got, "he should know making the Phantom whole again is impossible."

"All things are possible to he who holds the Great Eye."

"You mean *she*," the princess butted in belligerently. "So how come you're still here? I've been wishing you to hell for the last ten seconds."

"The Great Eye cannot hear you, Highness." Achmed gave her a piteous look. "It is weak and in pain, crying out for revenge and reunion. Once you and Mr. Sanquist have paid for your sacrilege, it will be whole again and strong and one with Allah."

Achmed had obviously been out in the desert sun too long. His tale was the weirdest mix of mysticism and death-to-the-infidels fundamentalism Chase had ever heard. The same kind of reactionary rhetoric had started the Crusades and sent Sir Ossric off to reclaim the Holy Land for Christendom. Not to mention steal the Phantom and kill Shehabi's ancestor the sultan. It sounded like so much new-age claptrap to Chase, but at least it explained Shehabi's fury over the brooch.

"What sacrilege?" the princess demanded.

"Recutting the stone," Chase said.

"I didn't recut it. Prince Sandor recut it."

"He's dead. You're not and you're a direct descendant."

"And you're a direct descendant of Sir Ossric." The princess blinked at him, stunned. "Well, this sucks."

"What's the going rate for sacrilege these days?" Chase asked Achmed. "The princess doesn't have her checkbook, but we salvaged some of the jewels from the vault."

"Sanquist!" the princess hissed at him furiously. Chase caught her fingers and gave them a shut-up squeeze.

"Only blood can undo what has been done." Achmed half raised his scimitar in both hands, a zealous gleam in his dark eyes. "My prince awaits to perform the ceremony that will restore the Great Eye."

The princess gulped.

"I guess it's what we deserve." Chase turned toward her and reached for the bag. She wrenched it away from him and clutched it to her hip. "What are you *doing?*"

"Throwing in the towel. We're done, finished, beat fair and square." Chase clamped a hand on the bag, yanked it and the princess toward him and ripped open the zipper.

She glared at him, chin quivering, eyes bright with angry, frightened tears. Chase ignored her and fished the scepter out of the bag. He carried it to Achmed and held it out to him on both hands.

"Hold this while I'll take off the brooch."

The Phantom glowed in the dim passageway, bathing the dank stone walls with a faint blue aura. Achmed gazed at it, eyes wide with wonder and reverence. He murmured what sounded like a prayer in Arabic and reached for it.

Holding his breath, Chase waited until his grip on the scimitar slackened, then closed his fingers around the scepter, drew back his arms and swung it with all his strength at Achmed's head. The Phantom cracked into his skull like a giant blue carbon baseball and felled him like a tree.

Chase jumped clear as the sword clattered to the stones and Achmed landed with a thump. He rolled on his back, out cold, jaw slack, eyes open and glazed. Chase poked him with one foot to make sure. He didn't so much as twitch.

"Is he dead?" the princess asked, sidling up beside him. A pulse beat visibly in the hollow of her throat above her dust-caked emerald necklace.

"I don't know and I don't care." Chase tucked the scepter in her bag, his arms shuddering from the shock of the blow, and zipped it. "Which way from here?"

"This way." She grabbed his hand and led him at a run around the left-hand curve in the passageway.

16

THE UPPER CHAMBERS of the dungeon lay dead ahead, their ancient stone walls and studded wooden doors flickering in the dull glow of a low-watt bulb hanging from a chain. The princess didn't stop to give Chase the five-franc tour, just raced past them and ducked into a small, dim passageway on the other side.

"Keep your head down and mind the channel in the floor," she tossed over her shoulder.

The edges of the shallow trough that ran more or less down the middle were eroded by time, blood and the charnel Chase knew had once been flushed this way out of the torture chambers behind them. He suppressed a chill, breathed cool, wet air and heard thunder rumble, the faint wail of a siren, and raised his flashlight from the floor.

Rain danced in the beam and lightning flickered beyond the circular opening just ahead. The princess slipped to a stop on stones made slick by blown-in rain and drew a shuddery breath in the cold, wet wind whistling past them into the passage.

"We're about a quarter of a mile below the palace. From here, we have to climb the rest of the way down outside."

She peered into the rain and shivered, gooseflesh springing on her arms. Chase undid the brooch, took off his plaid and wrapped it around her twice. "How far?" he asked, tying the ends together.

"About another quarter of a mile." She pulled a fold of the plaid over her head and arched an eyebrow as he snapped the brooch shut and tucked it in his sporran. "Don't you trust me to give it back?"

Chase kicked off his slick-soled dancing pumps and saw that one had lost a buckle. He tucked them in the waistband of his kilt and looked the princess in the eye. "Would you trust me to give the Phantom back?"

"When hell froze over."

"There you have it. I don't trust you any more than you trust me. I'll go first. Ready?"

She nodded and took a deep breath.

The hillside below was mostly jumbled rocks. Wet, muddy and slick. They slipped and slithered more than they climbed, and landed at the bottom soaked and covered with mud.

Chase was first to regain his feet on the flat, puddled verge of a weedy field and look back up the hill at the palace. He felt his stomach twist, but knew there was no way he could keep the princess from looking back, too.

She took the sight of leaping flames and black smoke billowing up to meet the storm clouds better than he expected. She didn't scream and she didn't try to kick him when she bolted and he grabbed her. She bit him instead, on the wrist, and tried to wrench away from him.

"Let me go! My mother and Danny will think I'm in there! They'll think I'm dead!"

"Listen to me." Chase thought about slapping her but opted for shaking her.

She stopped fighting and glared at him, her breast heaving, her hands balled into fists against his chest. His plaid had slipped off her head, and streaming tendrils of hair dripped down her cheeks.

"They'll think you're dead until the firemen don't find your charred remains," Chase told her bluntly. "That can't be helped, but if you really want to keep the Phantom out of your uncle and Shehabi's clutches and save your neck, we can use that time to get a good head start on them."

"What d'you mean, save my neck?"

Her problems had nothing to do with him, nothing at all, but she'd gotten him out of the vault alive. She deserved to know what was going on so she'd be able to take care of herself once he'd delivered her safely to the St. Cristobel embassy in Edinburgh. Sans the Phantom, of course.

"You didn't believe all that metaphysical claptrap Achmed spouted, did you?"

"Of course not. I'm a princess, not a fool." She pulled one hand away from him and angrily scraped her dripping hair out of her eyes. "I'm sure Achmed believed it, which is a very clever con on Shehabi's part to get him to kill me so he can put my uncle on the throne and rule St. Cristobel through him. What I don't know is why."

"He's a prince by birth and a gunrunner by profession. He needs a base to deliver the goods to his new clients in eastern Europe."

She tilted her head suspiciously. "How do you know?"

"Inspector Francis is working undercover for British Intelligence. They're working with the CIA to bag Shehabi."

"Did he know Shehabi meant to kill me?"

"The possibility had occurred to him."

"I see." The princess glanced at the burning palace, then at him, her chin notched up and only the slightest quaver in her bottom lip. "In that case, I think we should be going. I assume you have an escape route planned."

"A scathingly brilliant one, even if I do say so myself."

"Really. What is it?"

"We get on a plane and fly the hell out of here."

"Like this?" She arched an eyebrow and plucked at the mud-drenched folds of her gown.

"I assume you packed clothes as well as shoes."

"Well, yes, but—"

"Then you can change in the car."

"What car?" Molly asked, but Sanquist didn't answer. He grabbed her elbow and pulled her across the field.

It was littered with trash and like running on a sponge. The bag thumped against Molly's hip and she couldn't seem to stop shivering. The soaked plaid drooping off her shoulders didn't help. Neither did the sinking feeling she had that there was something very wrong with this picture.

She couldn't put her finger on what, exactly, but something had slipped out of gear. This wasn't her plan anymore. She was reacting rather than acting, could almost see herself dancing like a puppet to somebody else's tune. She didn't know the music or the steps, and she had no idea who was pulling her strings.

Three times Molly tripped and almost fell over the hem of her gown. Twice she almost jerked away from Chase Sanquist to run back to the palace. She had evidence enough to throw Shehabi out of St. Cristobel, but nothing concrete to connect him to her uncle. Inviting him to the ball was hardly proof of conspiracy to commit murder.

She was sure Shehabi had henchmen aplenty besides Achmed and Habib he could leave behind in St. Cristobel to do his bidding, and every confidence that Inspector Francis would be delighted to continue to use her as the lure to catch Shehabi. Sanquist hadn't said she was bait, but he didn't have to—she was a princess, not a fool.

And there was still the Phantom and the security of St. Cristobel to protect. Danny would die for her, Otto, too, and her mother, but she couldn't—*she wouldn't*—put them in that kind of danger. They'd be safer without her. Worried sick until they found out for sure she hadn't been caught in the fire or the bomb blast, but as Sanquist pointed out, that couldn't be helped. At least until she could find a phone.

The rain had nearly stopped by the time they reached a block of deserted brick warehouses edging the far side of the field and the dark, narrow street beyond. Puddles slicked with oil filled holes in the pavement, and only two of the street lamps on the whole block worked. The closest one cast a feeble gleam on the dull gray hood of a Fiat sedan parked near the mouth of an alley. Sanquist fished keys out of his sporran, unlocked the doors and opened the trunk.

"You can change in the car or in the alley." He opened a leather grip and stripped off his torn, sodden and filthy velvet jacket. "Just be quick about it."

"Where are you going to change?"

"Right here." He ripped off what had once been a white shirt with a lace jabot and cuffs and used it to scrub the mud off his face, hands and neck. The silk scraped against his whiskers. The dull, burnished gleam of lush, blond chest hair scraped against Molly's stretched and jangled nerves.

Before he could reach for the waistband of his kilt, she ducked into the alley. This was no time to find out what he did—or didn't—wear underneath it.

She was soaked to the skin, which meant changing her underwear. A tricky task hopping from one foot to the other. She tucked her jewelry in the bag, then used Sanquist's plaid as he'd used his shirt, the rough wool stimulating her in places that were already sensitized by the sight of him without a shirt. She shook her head, to wipe the image from her mind as much as to loosen the pins from her hair, and emerged from the alley in jeans and a dark sweater with a brush tucked in her pocket.

Sanquist sat on the back bumper in faded, stone-washed black jeans and a sweater that looked green in the poor light but which she thought was probably gray. He glanced up at her as he tied black, low-topped Nikes.

"You're fast. That's good." The tone of his voice said it surprised him.

"I can follow simple directions." Molly lifted the plaid and the ruined gown draped over her arm. "What about these?"

"Toss 'em in the trunk."

She did as he straightened off the car and picked up the brooch from the top of his grip. Molly felt a flash of irritation when he slipped it into his left front pocket before closing the bag and the trunk. She didn't say anything, just got into the car beside him as he slid behind the wheel and started the engine.

Molly tucked her bag beneath her knees and brushed her hair while he drove. If he noticed the tears in her eyes she'd point to the snarls in her hair. If he noticed how her hands shook, she'd tell him she was cold. If he asked if she'd changed her mind and wanted to go home, she'd say yes.

She hoped he wouldn't ask, hoped she had courage enough to pull this off. For the sake of her country and her own self-worth. If she could save the Phantom, maybe she *was* cut out to be a princess, after all. Maybe she wasn't the freaky, half-and-half hybrid she felt like most of the time. And if she was really lucky, maybe Sanquist would take his shirt off again before they parted company.

"How are we going to get the Phantom and the jewels I managed to salvage past Customs?" Molly asked.

"Don't worry about it, Princess. I'm an expert. You *did* bring your passport, didn't you?"

"Of course I did, but I don't have a ticket."

"I'll buy you one. You can pay me back."

"You have that much money on you?"

"No, but I have American Express."

The brush caught in her hair. Chase braked at a corner and glanced at her. She closed her mouth and blinked.

"It's a gold card," he said. "Wanna see it?"

"No." She looked out the side window and started brushing again. Furiously.

Chase smothered a grin. He'd tracked through enough back streets to make sure they weren't being tailed, turned left and merged the Fiat into a stream of traffic crawling toward the airport. With the casinos around the bay open all night, this late-hour crush wasn't uncommon. But the sawhorses thrown across the street a block or so ahead and the blue lights flashing behind them were impossible.

"Hell's bells."

Molly wheeled her head around, saw the checkpoint ahead, and felt her heart plummet to her toes. "Those are palace guards. Get us out of here."

Chase had already nudged the Fiat into the outside lane. Courteously, with the turn signal flashing. Still the driver of the Peugeot behind him took it personally and laid on the horn. The guards making a car-by-car search raised their heads and craned their necks.

Under his breath, Chase told the Peugeot driver what he could do with himself, cut the wheel hard left and trod on the gas. In the rearview mirror, he saw one guard snap a walkie-talkie off his belt while the other ran to the checkpoint, waving his arms.

"They made us," he said, wheeling the Fiat into an alley, its tires screaming at only forty miles an hour.

"Now what?" Molly asked nervously.

"Now we wish to God I'd rented a Ferrari," Chase said, and pushed the pedal harder.

The Fiat sprang forward like its engine had just sprouted four more cylinders. Not quite like a Ferrari, but close enough to make Chase think he'd underestimated the sedate little sedan. He made another hard left out of the alley onto a side street, the tires squealing nicely.

"I thought you said we'd get a head start," the princess said, looking out the back window.

"We should have. See what's on the radio." Chase saw a flash of whipping blue lights turning out of the alley behind them and cranked the wheel right into another one.

A very narrow and cobbled alley. Dumpsters loomed dangerously close and trash flew up around the tires. The princess bumped him with her shoulder as she leaned forward and pushed buttons searching for a news program.

She found one as Chase screeched the Fiat left into another street, two more alleys, then a locked-up commercial side street, the headlights glaring on glass storefronts covered with black mesh grills. In rapid French, a newscaster announced that Her Serene Highness had been kidnapped during a terrorist bomb attack on the palace. All ports of entry into St. Cristobel were closed by order of the Regent, and a massive hunt for the princess, still believed to be in San Blanco, was underway.

"Goddamn him!" Her Serene Highness screeched furiously. "How does he know where I am?"

"I wish I knew," Chase said, just as a squad car shot into the intersection ahead and came at them skidding sideways on the wet street. "Get down."

He flung the princess by her shoulder onto the floor. She cracked her head on the dashboard but tucked herself up underneath it. Playing chicken at crosswalks was one thing, playing chicken with a car doing fifty was something else, yet Chase aimed the Fiat at the whirling blue lights bearing down on them. He held his breath until the guard behind the wheel slammed on his brakes and swung the car toward the sidewalk, then he stomped the gas pedal and rocketed the Fiat through the intersection.

More blue lights appeared two blocks ahead. Chase swore viciously under his breath and screamed the Fiat into another alley. How in hell were they managing to get ahead of him? He'd lost the guards from the checkpoint six blocks ago, done enough zigging and zagging and backtracking to flummox any attempt at triangulating a projected course. If he didn't know better, he'd swear they had a bug on him.

He glanced at the princess as he fought the Fiat through a fishtailing right turn onto a dim, deserted back street bordering the seedier west end of town. She was rubbing her head. Not the right side she'd thumped on the dash, but the left. The same spot she'd scratched during the ball and in the vault.

"Did you bring your coronet with you?"

"Yes," she said, peering at him over her knees tucked under her chin.

"Give it to me and turn on the dash light."

She didn't ask why, just scrambled onto the seat and did it. Chase eased back on the accelerator, steering with his knees while he flipped the coronet over and peeled away the strip of velvet padding on the inside.

"Look here." He held the coronet up in his right hand and showed the princess the bug affixed to the inside edge. "Here's how your uncle knows exactly where you are."

She blinked, stunned, then gritted her jaw. "I'll kill him."

"I'll help you," Chase said grimly, careening the Fiat through another turn and flooring the accelerator.

It took him six more blocks and eight more alleys, flashing past intersections filled with spinning blue lights, dogged by the faint wail of sirens closing in behind them, to find what he was looking for—a garbage truck blocking half the street as it backed up to empty a Dumpster sitting in the mouth of an alley.

Chase rolled down his window, laid on the horn and aimed the Fiat at the hydraulic drum slowly rolling open on the back end of the truck. He hoped to God the driver could hear him over the rumble, pushed the pedal to the floor and shot the Fiat into the narrowing gap between truck and Dumpster. He flung the coronet into the half-open maw, heard it land with a clunk, then swung the wheel hard left to avoid a head-on collision with the corner of a dingy gray brick building.

It was a near miss, sparks flying as the right side door scraped the facade. Chase eased off the gas and cut the wheel again. The Fiat bounced off the curb into the street, skidded through an about-face turn and shot into an alley on the opposite side.

"Where in hell," the princess asked, her voice unnaturally calm, "did you learn to drive?"

"The highlands of Scotland, Highness." Chase shot her a grin, his heart pumping with excitement as the wail of the sirens began to fade behind them.

The Fiat screeched out of the alley onto a four-lane boulevard. On the center island, ornamental trees strung with white lights glittered like diamonds. When a bilingual sign welcoming tourists to San Blanco, the capital of St. Cristobel, flashed past, Chase relaxed and eased off the gas pedal.

"If you don't mind, I'll call you Chase from now on," the princess said. "And I think you should call me Molly."

"Why's that?"

"Because," she said, turning her head to look at him, "I'm about to throw up in your lap."

17

SHE TUCKED HER HEAD between her knees instead, wrapped her hands around her shins and stayed there so long Chase thought she'd fallen asleep. He'd put twenty miles of suburbs between them and San Blanco when she straightened and raked her hair back with her fingers.

"How do you suppose my uncle found out about Plan C?" she said. "I didn't tell anybody. Not even Danny."

"I don't think he knew about Plan C, the bomb threat or the bug in your coronet. I think that was all Shehabi. He wanted to make sure you were in the right place at the right time to be blown to bits."

"How did he put that thing in my coronet, d'you suppose?"

"I'd suppose he's got somebody inside the palace."

"That's what I thought." The princess unzipped her bag and took out a flashlight and the royal scepter.

She laid it on her lap and turned on the dash light. Dim as the bulb was, it set fire to the Phantom, filling the car with a soft blue glow and swelling the murmur inside Chase's head.

"What are you doing?" he asked, wiggling the tip of one finger in his ear.

"Making sure he didn't put a bug in the scepter."

Why hadn't he thought of that? He *should* have. Maybe he *would* have if the damned buzzing in his head would stop. It was beginning to get on his nerves and make it difficult to concentrate.

"Very good, Princess," Chase said, relieved that she'd thought of it, yet annoyed that he hadn't.

"Molly," she replied, gripping the scepter in both hands and turning the bottom of it counterclockwise. "There's a hidey-hole here where Prince Sandor kept his poisons."

The platinum-crusted end càp came off in her hand. She laid it on the dash and shone the light inside. As the Fiat topped a hill, Chase heard the faint wail of sirens behind them. So did the princess. She flashed him a wide-eyed look, plucked a second bug, no bigger than a watch battery, out of the scepter and held it up between the first two fingers of her left hand.

"Shehabi is really starting to piss me off," Chase said grimly, and punched the accelerator.

The Fiat's headlights flashed past a sign marking the entrance to the village of Alisandria. Arrows pointed up, down, left and right, giving directions to tourist sites and services. Chase followed the arrow leading to an all-night gas station, sliding the Fiat through a wet and slick right-hand curve.

"Gimme the bug," he said to the princess. "Put the scepter back in the bag and get out of sight."

The sirens were getting closer, close enough to make Molly's heart pound as the Fiat wheeled into a filling station. She scrunched herself under the dashboard again. She caught a glimpse of a red Jaguar idling at the pumps, saw Sanquist roll down his window, then nothing but muddy floor mat as he gave her a push on the top of her head.

She heard a metallic ping, spat carpet fuzz and raised her head. Sanquist was rolling up his window, the filling station lights falling away behind them.

"What did you do with the bug?"

"Tossed it in a trash can."

"Oh, *good*." Molly sighed with relief, then winced and glanced at Sanquist. He was frowning at her.

"What did you think I did with it?"

"I'd rather not say. Can I come out of here?"

"No." He made a sharp left that knocked her off balance and bumped her right shoulder against the door. "I'm not your uncle and I'm not Alec Tremayne. I don't hurt people."

"What do you call stealing?"

"A necessity of life."

"A job is a necessity of life." Molly grabbed the seat belt buckle, pulled herself up on her knees and blew her hair out of her eyes. "Why don't you get one?"

"Why don't you?"

"I've got a job." Molly crawled into the seat and glared at him. "I'm a princess."

"That's an accident of birth." Sanquist made a right onto the deserted village square. "Some of us aren't so fortunate."

"I'd say a gold American Express card was pretty fortunate. Or did you steal it?"

In front of the gingerbread-trimmed town hall, Sanquist slammed on the brakes, shoved the gear shift into Park and opened his door, grabbed Molly's left wrist and dragged her out of the car behind him. She clamped her right hand around the steering wheel, but he pried her fingers loose and yanked her, flat-footed and falling, onto the wet pavement.

Her Reeboks saved her from splashing facefirst in a muddy puddle, the perfect place for her hoity-toity little highness. Chase hadn't been this angry since he'd punched Tony, since he'd flung Queen Victoria's cup out of Jean-Marc's hand. There was a connection there, something his brain tried to tell him but couldn't through the blue-white fury blazing through him.

He grabbed the princess by her right elbow and wrenched her around to face the town hall. A green and black ribbon wishing her happy birthday in French fluttered across the facade in a snatch of cool, wet breeze.

"I don't get banners on my birthday," he told her. "I get tax bills from Inland Revenue telling me to pay up or vacate a castle I'm lucky I see twice a year, bills for new roofs, bills to replace old plumbing rotting out of the walls, bills for heating oil in the winter. Bills the postman has to lift with both hands."

"You aren't alone." The princess twisted free and spun on one foot, her eyes flashing in the backwash of the floodlights illuminating the front of the building. "I lost a whole wing of my palace tonight, God knows how many priceless antiques, state treasures and the jewels my uncle stole!"

"Poor little princess. Now you know how it feels to get ripped off."

She slapped him. Hard enough to snap his neck and quiet the blood-thumping roar in his head. Chase heard the sirens wailing closer, rubbed his stinging cheek and wondered what the hell was wrong with him, why in hell they were standing here in the street shouting at each other.

"Thanks for the lift." The princess swept past him and yanked her bag out of the car. She dumped it on the hood, dug out a wad of twisted jewelry and threw it at him. "For your time and trouble, Mr. Sanquist."

Molly looped the bag over her shoulder and wheeled away. She'd never been so angry or so humiliated in her life. She didn't know where she was going, or which one of them was the bigger fool. She'd taken no more than three steps when the sirens died and she heard a rapid burst of ratta-ratta gunfire. It echoed across the square from the direction of the filling station, froze the breath in her throat and her feet to the pavement.

If the guards were trying to save her from a kidnapper, why were they shooting?

She heard brakes squeal, gears grind, and spun around as Sanquist backed the Fiat up beside her, leaned across the seat and pushed the door open. "C'mon, Princess. Let's go."

Molly dove into the car and slammed the door. Sanquist punched the gas and switched off the headlights, and the Fiat shot away into a narrow side street. Clutching the bag in one hand, the armrest on the door with the other, Molly held her breath as dark, square shapes she figured were houses slipped by on both sides of the car.

She had no idea how Sanquist could see, how he knew where he was going, or why, why, *why* the guards had been shooting. Unless they weren't palace guards. Unless they were more of Shehabi's kinsmen in palace guard uniforms. That made sense. It also meant Shehabi had his fingers into the day-to-day running of her country. Big time.

She couldn't think about that, not now—not without screaming—so she thought about Chase Sanquist and what he'd told her. It made her cheeks burn, but she thought about it and asked, "Why do you get the tax bills? Your cousin's the earl."

"Tony's side of the family only inherited the title, not the land. Glyco is mine. Or it will be when my uncle Cosmo's gone."

Sanquist made a deft right-hand swing around a split-rail fence and accelerated the Fiat down a muddy, graveled lane that ran parallel with the highway. Molly caught glimpses of wet blacktop and occasional headlights through the trees on the left side.

"Your passport says you're American."

"I am. So was my mother." He switched on the lights and adjusted the rearview mirror. "I think we lost 'em."

For now, Molly thought. "You don't want to talk to me, do you?" she asked.

Chase wondered how she knew that, if she knew he wanted to kiss her and if she could tell him why. "Not especially," he said. "Unless you've got an idea for getting us the hell out of St. Cristobel with the borders closed."

"Actually I think I might," Molly said slowly. "My father's hunting *schloss.* It's a royal game preserve, really. Four hundred acres of prime St. Cristobel forest that just happen to march with the French border."

"Don't tell me." Sanquist veered the Fiat around a left-hand curve, up a muddy hill, and shot her a sour, sideways look. "Nobody else knows about it."

"Don't be ridiculous. Everybody knows about it, but there aren't any border checkpoints."

Sanquist arched a dubious eyebrow. "None?"

"Nary a one. St. Cristobel has never been a threat—well, not since Bonaparte—so the French could care less, and my father simply wouldn't allow checkpoints and guards on the compound."

"That hardly seems strategically bright."

"Oh, it wasn't, but it definitely made it easier for him to sneak in and out with his mistress."

She said it in such a deadpan voice Chase thought she was kidding. He almost laughed, until he glanced at her and saw the look on her face, the shadow that had nothing to do with the reflection of the dashboard lights.

The Fiat made the crest of the hill, its tires spinning mud. The highway lay just ahead. Chase stopped the car and looked at the princess. "How far?"

She leaned forward, looking up and pointing due north at the shadowed bulk of wooded foothills below the mountains it was too dark to see on the far horizon.

"About two hundred miles thataway. Straight up."

Chase pressed the light on his watch. Two-seventeen.

"How are the roads between here and there?"

"Narrow as a donkey path, chock-full of blind curves and hairpin switchbacks," she said, turning her head to look at him. "You'll be right at home."

Chase wanted to smile but didn't. She'd smile back and that could be dangerous, a complication neither one of them needed. They were in enough trouble already. He withdrew the clump of tangled jewelry she'd thrown at him from under his sweater and tossed it in her lap.

"Let's get a couple things straight, Princess. We need to switch cars. We can't risk renting one and leaving a paper trail, so I'll have to steal one. That's what I do. I'm a thief, and a damned good one. Try to remember that's the reason you sought me out in the first place, and keep your moral outrage to yourself."

"I apologize," she said, turning sideways in the seat to look at him. "You're absolutely right. There's no excuse for what I said. I'm sorry. It won't happen again."

Her eyes looked very bright in the semidarkness, too bright, but they held his squarely. Her chin quavered only once, then she had it under control. Which was more than Chase could say for the stab of guilt he felt and the pulse-thumping need to touch her and tell her everything would be all right. As easily as lies had always come to him, he couldn't bear the thought of lying to her now.

"Make sure it doesn't," he said instead, clamping his hands around the steering wheel. "Now let's go find a Ferrari."

18

CHASE SETTLED FOR a three-year-old Land Rover in the next village with a full tank of gas, an infinitely more practical vehicle for what lay ahead. The princess helped him shift their gear from the Fiat, then dutifully drove it behind him out of town and helped him hide it halfway down an overgrown tractor path leading to a rain-mucked cow pasture.

By the time they finished they were both filthy, the princess staggering with exhaustion and pale beneath the mud on her face. Chase had her mark the route on the map the rental company provided with the Fiat, then gave her a gentle push into the back of the Rover. She was asleep before her head hit the seat. He tossed his mostly dry plaid over her, headed the Land Rover north at five miles above the speed limit, and realized he'd made two colossal mistakes.

Shehabi couldn't possibly have planted both bugs; it simply stretched credulity too far. More than likely Inspector Francis had put the one in the coronet. Knowing Shehabi wanted the princess dead, he'd taken every precaution against losing track of her—until Chase tossed the coronet into the garbage truck.

That meant the guards who'd chased them through San Blanco were probably the inspector's men, and the thugs who'd shot up the gas station were Shehabi's. If he'd been paying attention, if he hadn't been distracted by the racket still going on in his head, he would have—*and he should have*—realized all this in San Blanco. He could've left the princess there for Inspector Francis to scoop up in his safety net and gotten away clean with the Phantom.

That was his first mistake. His second was adjusting the rearview mirror so he could watch her sleep. His third was murmuring, "Molly," very softly under his breath.

A silly name, but it suited her. It wouldn't when she was a seventy-five-year-old white-headed Dowager Princess with another man's children and grandchildren clustered around her arthritic knees. If she lived that long, if he didn't get them both killed before they crossed the border.

If the incessant murmur in his head didn't drive him nuts first, Chase thought he might be able to pull it off. He prayed it would stop, swore if it did he wouldn't touch her, vowed he'd be content to watch her Diamond Jubilee on TV at Glyco, a shawl over his lap, a bowl of gruel in his hand. He promised he wouldn't wonder what might have happened if he'd taken her when he'd wanted to, swore on everything he held dear that he wouldn't give either one of them anything to regret.

Ah, but that was the rub. Besides Cosmo, Glyco and that old rascal Jean-Marc, there wasn't a hell of a lot Chase held dear. He'd never had the time or the inclination. Why he did now when he didn't have the time was, he supposed, just one of life's little gotchas. One best left unexplored.

While it was still good and dark, Chase found another all-night gas station on the fringe of the foothills and topped the tank in the Land Rover. The attendant was tired and irritable. Chase gave him something to remember, a loud-mouthed tourist in dark glasses and a Chicago Bears baseball cap, who bitched about the price of coffee to go in godawful French with a Texas accent.

When dawn began to push up the slopes through the right side window and the princess began to murmur in her sleep, Chase found a turnaround and pulled into it. He wasn't tired or hungry, but that wasn't unusual. He'd conditioned himself to run on adrenaline when he had to. Still he drank one of the cups of coffee he'd bought and ate a tasteless cherry Danish.

He crumpled the cup and wrapper, took off the princess' cap and lifted her bag from the floor to put it back. The Phantom winked at him atop the scepter and a wrinkled pair of jeans. He took it out, propped it against the steering wheel and watched the stone catch fire in the first light of day.

He knew how to pop it out of the scepter, by twisting the diamond-studded ring of rubies beneath the crown piece counterclockwise, but didn't. He didn't want the princess to know he knew that little trick. He simply sat and gazed at it, marveling at its beauty, its color—its worth—and then he touched it.

Just barely, hardly grazed more than his thumbnail against it, and felt the murmur in his head crash like surf on a beach at high tide, his breath catch and his heart seize, saw colors he'd never imagined existed, exquisite, three-dimensional colors he knew were as impossible as the images swirling inside them. Things never meant to have form or substance—his deepest fears and darkest desires—took shape in front of him and began to breathe, to beat with his heart, to pound with his blood . . .

Molly jerked awake, heart thudding, eyes wide and staring. Bad dream, she thought sleepily, though she couldn't remember it. Thank God. Every inch of her ached, every muscle creaked, as she stretched on the cold vinyl seat and pushed herself up on one arm, yawning and blinking, and saw Chase Sanquist slumped and sound asleep behind the wheel.

She yawned again and stretched, drew a deep breath and smelled coffee, peeked over the back of the front seat and saw three plastic cups leaking steam through their lids inside a white paper sack. And a Danish. A blueberry Danish. Her favorite.

"Oh, what a beautiful morning," Molly said.

She whispered it so she wouldn't wake him, but he jumped like she'd blown a bugle in his ear, whipped his head around and flung out his arms. She ducked and narrowly missed getting whacked in the nose with the back of his hand, saw his eyes were wide open and saw the scepter topple off the steering wheel onto the floor.

He sucked air into his lungs, a deep, shuddery gasp like he'd been holding his breath, and blinked at her. She didn't realize until then that his pupils were fixed and dilated.

"Sorry," he mumbled, rubbing his eyes. "I must've dozed off."

His voice sounded deep and dreamy, but his hand was trembling. He was pale, too, his whiskered jaw almost the same color as his sweater, which Molly could see now *was* gray, as gray as the morning light seeping into the Land Rover. Both were symptoms of fatigue. Still, she thought it was odd.

"Would you mind terribly putting that back where it belongs?" she asked, nodding an arched eyebrow at the scepter.

I plan to, Chase thought, but said, "Certainly." He picked it up, put it back with her Bears cap, zipped the bag shut and swung it onto the floor. Then he slid behind the wheel and shifted into Reverse.

"Wait a second," the princess said.

Chase did, while she climbed over the seat, wrapped his plaid around her shoulders, flipped on the heater and balanced the coffee bag between her knees.

"I never get to ride in front." She took out a cup and peeled off the lid as he backed the Rover out of the turnaround and headed up the mountain. "Do you always sleep with your eyes open?"

"I wouldn't know." Chase gave her a sharp, sideways look.

He hoped she wouldn't, but she asked, "Mrs. Sanquist has never mentioned it?"

He should've said, "Every night before we tuck our twelve kids into bed." It would've been kinder to both of them if he had, but he looked at her again and said, "I'm not married."

"Oh." She ducked her head and sipped her coffee, a soft *aha* smile lifting the corner of her mouth.

Chase waited until she swallowed, then asked, "Do you want to have sex?"

She splashed coffee on her knee, changed hands with her cup, wiped her fingers on her jeans and said, "Do I *what?*"

"Do you want to have sex?" He glanced at her again as he nosed the Rover one-handed through a curve. "With me."

"Since you're the only other person in the car," she replied frostily, way, *way* up on her royal high horse, "I assumed that's what you meant."

"So do you or don't you?"

"Not that it's any of your business, Mr. Sanquist, but I have never had sex in my life."

"I didn't think so."

"I have, however, made love. Is that what you'd like to do with me?"

"*Hell*, no, I mean, no."

"I didn't think so," she said, and looked out the window.

"I didn't mean to offend you. I was just trying to establish some perimeters."

"You needn't bother." She gave him an affronted glare, a red stain spreading up her throat above the ribbed collar of her mud-splashed black sweater. "I have no designs on your body, Mr. Sanquist. I was curious about you, that's all. It was something to think about besides the fact that my uncle and a sheikh who fancies himself a sorcerer are trying to kill me."

"Then I'm sorry. But I thought—"

Her eyes went suddenly wide and she dove for the floor, spilling the coffee in her hand and the two others in the white sack. Over the whack of her head on the dashboard, Chase heard the whup-whup-whup of a helicopter and felt his stomach clutch.

"Gimme your hat," he said, snatching his sunglasses off the seat.

She tossed him the cap and he put it on, resisting the urge to floor the accelerator. He slid the shades over his nose, turned his head and saw a blue and white chopper swooping across the deep gorge beyond the guardrail on the left side of the road, its rotor flashing in a stray ray of sunshine piercing the overcast sky.

There's never a blizzard around when you need one, Chase thought darkly. He didn't want anything major, just a nice little whiteout that would make flying impossible. He watched the chopper cruise the ribbon of narrow, two-lane highway twisting ahead around the flank of the mountain, saw it bank into a steep turn and wished the Land Rover was invisible.

"Do they see us?" the princess asked nervously.

"Sure they see us." Chase watched the chopper loop around to make another pass. "But with any luck they're still looking for a gray Fiat."

A strong gust of wind buffeted the Land Rover. Chase held the wheel steady, watched the chopper with one eye, the curve coming up with the other, and saw tiny white flakes begin to dance on the hood. Another blast of wind swooped down the mountain, swirling a thick curtain of white over the Land Rover and blotting out the road.

"Who says wishing won't make it so?" Chase watched the blue and white chopper dive into the gorge to escape the sudden storm, and switched on the headlights and the wipers.

"What's happening?" The princess scrambled up on her knees, one hand on the dash, the other on the seat, and looked out the windshield. "It's snowing!"

"Snowing, hell. It's a blizzard." Chase grinned happily, the wipers beating at high speed. "Helicopters can't fly in blizzards."

The princess eased herself gingerly onto the seat, swung her bag into the back, then cocked her head at him curiously. "You wished it would snow and it did?"

"No, I didn't wish it, I—"

Yes, he had—no, he hadn't. He'd *thought* about snow, and he'd *wished* the Land Rover was invisible. He looked at the furious white gale swirling against the windshield, realized he'd gotten exactly what he'd wished for and felt a chill crawl up the back of his neck.

"It's just an expression," he said curtly. "And a lucky break for us."

Then why the leave-it-alone snap in his voice and the muscle twitching in his jaw? Molly wondered but didn't ask. She picked up a napkin from the seat, wiped her hands and looked mournfully at her blueberry Danish, awash in a sea of coffee on the floor.

She sighed, still hungry and thirsty, and settled herself Indian-style on the seat. She felt that odd, slipped-gear sensation again as a green and black on silver sign declaring the entrance to the Royal St. Cristobel Wildlife and Game Preserve swirled past in a billow of snow.

"We're here," she said. "Do you think anybody else is?"

"If they were, they wouldn't have bothered sending the chopper."

"I wonder how far they are behind us."

Chase wondered how close, hoped the snow would slow them down. He didn't wonder if they were there—he could feel them in the slow crawl up the back of his neck. He just wasn't sure *who* they were.

"You're certain the caretaker and his wife keep to the *schloss?*" he asked. "You're positive no one will be at the gamekeeper's cottage?"

"It's highly unlikely. Mrs. Schmidt cleans the cottage at the end of the month. This is the eighteenth. If we go in the back gate like I said, no one should see us."

Maybe no one should, but somebody might. The thought came unbidden into Chase's head, along with another warning chill up his spine as he cruised the Land Rover past the black iron main gates. Through the snow and a screen of bare tree branches, he saw four capped brick chimneys and the slate roof of the *schloss*. Some hunting lodge.

The back entrance to the compound lay around three more looping curves in the road, about a mile or so from the *schloss*. Chase stopped the Rover in front of a smaller black iron gate. He looked at the electronic number pad on the lock, felt gooseflesh and caught the princess by the elbow as she started to open her door.

"Is there another way in?"

"There's a service road a couple miles farther."

"Another gate?"

"No, just a chain. We'll have to walk about a mile to the cottage."

"Good. We'll go in that way."

Chase expected her to squawk, but she didn't, only sighed and rewrapped his plaid around her shoulders. Cosmo would say she had bottom. Cosmo loved women with bottom. She'd had a rotten night and a five-mile hike to the French border ahead of her, but she hadn't complained once.

It was just one of the reasons Chase wished she wasn't a princess and he wasn't a thief. He wondered what else she was, too, besides a great dancer and hopelessly above his touch. And he wished—God, how he wished—Chastain Sanquist had stayed the hell in Scotland, that he hadn't gone haring off to St. Cristobel in 1786 to lose his head and lose the title.

When they reached the service road, Chase got out and lowered the chain. The princess drove the Land Rover over it and parked it where he pointed, behind a stand of young oaks that still had last year's leaves. While she collected their gear and replaced the chain, Chase disconnected the ignition he'd hot-wired and erased the Land Rover's tracks with a pine branch. As hard as it was snowing, he figured the brush strokes would be buried in twenty minutes.

He took his grip from the princess, she shouldered her bag, and off they went. She only stopped once, to show him the hiking trail that twisted up the mountain to the French border, then led him the rest of the way through the snow toward the gamekeeper's cottage.

It was an A-frame built halfway up a ridge overlooking the *schloss,* well-hidden from open view by a screen of snow-dusted pines. The perfect place to hide a mistress.

Or seduce a princess and steal her diamond.

19

CHASE WAS NO LONGER SURE which he wanted more, the Phantom or the princess. He thought licking the snowflakes off her eyelashes would be a good way to find out, and he might have, if she hadn't made a beeline for the door straight across the small clearing behind the cottage.

He caught her arm and pulled her back, then led her in a zigzag course from tree to tree that would look random from the air, just in case the storm stopped and the chopper came back before the snow filled in their footprints.

On the flagstone patio outside the door, he dropped to his heels, opened his grip and said, "Be ready to duck inside and shut the alarm off."

Molly watched him unzip a small black leather case and take out a silver tool that looked to her like a crochet hook. "You can open a dead bolt with that?"

"I can open any lock in the world with this," he said, and did so, almost before he finished the sentence.

The bolt slid back with a thunk and Chase pushed the door open. Molly slipped inside and raced past the pool table where her mother had caught her father making love to another woman. She opened the garage door, punched the disarm code into the security panel on the wall behind it with twenty seconds to spare, then stepped inside the game room.

Chase stood beside the table, rolling the white cue ball into the corner pocket. "A very inventive fellow, Prince

Alisander," he said, with a rakish smile and cocked eyebrow.

Molly wished she hadn't told him the story, wondered fleetingly if it was the reason he'd made that stupid pass at her. She hadn't meant to tell him, she'd just sort of blurted it out while in terror of being arrested for car theft.

"He took the wild in wildlife preserve literally," she said, "until my mother caught him."

Chase shook his head and dropped the cue ball back in the pocket. "I can't imagine any man cheating on Natalie."

"Neither could she, and my father couldn't understand why she couldn't understand. Most men in St. Cristobel have a mistress. It's a European macho thing, but in Chicago it's a surefire ticket to divorce court."

She smiled, trying to make light of it, but her eyes were shadowed again and unhappy. Chase decided his plan to take her and the Phantom would have to wait until they crossed the border. Since the racket in his head was still going strong, all bets were off. So was his promise not to touch her. If he was going to go nuts, he was going to go happy, except for wondering who else she'd made love with and when.

He was going to take the Phantom, but not without giving her something to remember, something that would still give her hot flashes on her Diamond Jubilee.

No matter what she said, she wanted him. The faint flush on her throat and the fact that she couldn't quite look him in the eye told him so. And excited him. Only slightly more than he wanted to spread-eagle her on the pool table, he wanted to be away from here and from the nonstop crawl up the back of his neck. So he asked her, "Where are the backpacks you told me about?"

"In the garage, in the storage locker on the far wall."

"I'll get them and meet you in the kitchen." He started for the door, and she headed for the stairs leading to the main level. "Fine," she said. "I'll take a shower and—"

"No shower." Chase turned toward her with his hand on the knob. "There isn't time."

"I'm filthy, and I'm fast," she reminded him, swiveling on the third step with a stubborn look on her face. "You said so yourself."

"We came here for food, water and warm clothes," he said as he opened the door. "We don't have time for showers."

"Maybe *you* don't," Molly muttered, as he disappeared into the garage, "but *I* do."

Then she marched up the stairs, past the floor-to-ceiling windows and the telescope trained on the *schloss* where her father had sat and kept watch for her mother. She found a flannel-lined beige shooting jacket of his for Chase, and a green down jacket, cap and gloves she'd forgotten she owned.

She carried them into the great room, dumped them on a chair, turned toward the bathroom and stopped, glancing over her shoulder at the telescope. Maybe she ought to look, just in case. The way her luck was running, her prince would come and she'd be in the shower. He sure as hell wasn't in the garage looking for backpacks.

It was still snowing hard, which made focusing the lens tricky. When she did, she almost stopped breathing at the sight of a gray Rolls limo sweeping up to the rear entrance of the *schloss*. When the driver opened the door and her uncle got out, she did, for a dizzying half second, then she scooped up the coats and bolted for the stairs.

"Chase!" she screamed, racing down them so fast she lost her balance. If he hadn't caught her at the bottom, she would've landed on her face.

"Uncle Karroll—he's here," Molly blurted, her heart pumping in her throat. "I saw him through my father's telescope."

"Is Shehabi with him?"

"I don't know. I didn't wait around to see."

"Put your coat on and get out of here." Chase tossed the backpacks aside, swung her bag off her shoulder, took the down jacket from her and shoved her into it. "I'll catch up with you."

"No!" Molly spun after him and clutched his left wrist in both hands as he started up the stairs.

"We have to know if Shehabi's here, and we have to keep the Phantom safe." He turned to her and pried her fingers loose. "You showed me the trail. I'll catch up with you. Follow the footsteps we made and get going."

Molly stood for a second, stunned and stricken, at the foot of the stairs. Not run for your life, my brave little darling, just get the Phantom out of here. The diamond, the goddamned, God-cursed diamond.

The fact that he was right only hurt more, only made her angrier. She'd get the Phantom out of here, all right, herself with it, and to hell with him. Molly snatched up her bag, flung it over her shoulder and went.

She followed their half-filled footprints into the trees, then broke for the trail. The snow ate sound, and so did the cap she tugged on with the gloves. She thought about taking it off but didn't, opting for warmth and relying on sight.

The trail switched back and forth up the ridge like a cross-country ski track, which made the climb relatively easy. It was steep only in stretches and slick only in places where the ground was mostly rock.

Anger fueled Molly through the first couple of miles, until the snow began to taper off and the wind switched, tearing straight down the mountain and right in her teeth. She tugged Chase's plaid out from under her jacket and looped it around her face. It smelled like wet wool, mud and male.

She slogged on with her head bowed, telling herself the tears in her eyes were only because of the wind, until the weight of the jewels in her bag began to slow her down. She paused to rest and reconnoiter then, roughly halfway up the ridge, where the track leveled off on a wide ledge. The withered grass sprouting in icy tussocks between the rocks crunched beneath her feet and the bag she swung off her shoulder and dropped.

Molly wished she'd thought to pack food. Her knees were trembling, her head throbbing. What she wouldn't give for the cheeseburger she hadn't wanted last night. She was thirsty, too, her throat raw and aching with cold. The snow had stopped, and what she could see of the drifted, tree-hemmed trail behind her was empty.

Guilt and worry swamped her. What if Shehabi had come with her uncle? What if they'd caught Chase or he'd lost his way? What if he was looking for her behind every tree? What if she never saw him again, never got the chance to tell him that even if that's all he wanted, she'd have sex with him?

It wasn't what she wanted, and it sure as hell wasn't what she'd planned. Chase Sanquist had been a means to an end, a quick, sure ticket out of St. Cristobel with the Phantom. She hadn't planned on spending this much time with him, feeling her pulse race whenever he looked at her or shivering every time he touched her. Everything she'd planned had gone out the window. And maybe, just maybe, her heart, too.

"What kept you?" Chase said behind her.

He hoped he didn't sound like he was gasping for breath, even though he was. It was damn cold up here, the chill factor in the wind shrieking down the mountain face lowering the temperature a good twenty degrees. If she hadn't stopped he never would have caught her—forget sneaking around ahead of her—though God knew he'd been trying for the last hour and a half.

He wanted to throttle her for bolting like a scared rabbit, until she turned around and he realized she wasn't frightened. She was mad as hell, which was convenient, since he was, too. Her gloved hands were balled into fists and her eyes were as green as her forest down jacket.

"Since you're so worried about the Phantom," she said, her voice muffled by the plaid she'd wrapped over her mouth and nose, "you carry it for a while. It's heavy."

She slung the bag at him, hard, and stalked past him. Chase caught it against his chest, felt a dizzy rush and the nagging murmur swell inside his head. He shook it off, looped the bag over his arm with the backpack he'd stuffed the contents of his grip into, and wheeled after her.

"I told you I'd catch up with you." He grabbed her arm and swung her around to face him. "I did not tell you to leave me in the dust."

"Like you plan to do to me just as soon as we cross the border?" She lifted her elbow out of his hand, her chin and her cold-reddened cheeks from the folds of her plaid. "You think I don't know that?"

So that's what this is, Chase thought, watching tears jewel in her lashes. She had glorious lashes, thick and lush as the wind-whipped tendrils of gold-brown hair that had escaped her cap. They fluttered across her mouth but she tugged them away with a shaky hand and notched up her chin, daring him to deny it.

Twelve hours ago he would have, in a heartbeat. He still could, only it would be a lie, a lie that would land them both in the world of hurt he saw brimming in her eyes.

"Then why did you give me the Phantom?"

"Because it's all I have that you want," she retorted, twisting her arm free.

The tremble in her chin made his heart wrench. So much for lies, he thought, and said, "You're wrong."

"The hell I am. You'd do or say anything to get your hands on the Phantom."

"You bet I would. Anything but this," he said, dropping both bags and grabbing her.

The rough kiss he clamped on her mouth didn't surprise Molly. She'd seen it coming, but she didn't care. She hadn't planned on wanting him to touch her, to hold her, to tell her she was anything but the scared little coward she felt like. But she did, even if it was a lie.

It wasn't a lie, it was a mistake. Chase knew it the instant their lips met. He'd meant to be rough, to scare her, to make her hate him and think he was a brute, but it wasn't working. Her cold, wind-chapped lips were warming and softening beneath his, her arms creeping around his neck. He caught her wrists and backed away from her, the murmur in his head soaring, her eyes glistening.

"This is trouble," he said. The unsteady edge in his voice surprised him, sent the warning chill shooting up the back of his neck. "Trouble neither one of us needs."

"Why? Because I'm a princess?"

"No. Because I'm a thief."

"You could change."

"I don't want to. Not even for you."

The glimmer went out of her eyes. So did the quaver in her chin. It wasn't what Chase wanted. He wanted her and he wanted the Phantom. He couldn't have both, yet he couldn't seem to make up his mind which he wanted more.

Forcing her to choose was a low, sleazy trick, but he was a low, sleazy guy, so he said, "This isn't just something I do, it's what *I* am. I was born to it, like you were born to be a princess. I enjoy it. I get off on it. It's better than sex."

He expected her to slap him again, but she didn't. Just pulled her wrists out of his hands and backed away from him.

"Then I'm just making it easy for you, aren't I?" she said, and wheeled away from him.

Molly stalked away up the trail, hoping he'd follow her, but knowing he wouldn't. He had what he wanted and so did she, proof positive that she wasn't cut out to be a princess. She'd failed her country, her father's memory and every Savard who'd ever ruled St. Cristobel.

And she couldn't care less. She'd tell the story she'd heard on the radio, that Chase had kidnapped her and stolen the Phantom. She'd never tell anyone, not even her mother, that she'd given it to him along with her heart.

Molly wished she could take it back, wished she'd never met him. More than anything she wished he hadn't kissed her in the vault. That's when she'd fallen for him, when he'd swung her off the hook. Not that he cared.

A fierce gust of wind howled past her, whipping the trees lining the ledge and showering Molly with icy snow. A branchful slid down her collar and made her gasp. So did Chase when he spun her around and gripped both her arms.

"We made a deal, Princess. You'd get me out of the vault and I'd get you and the Phantom out of St. Cristobel. We're a couple miles short of that, so you're stuck with me. Like it or not."

Over the whoosh of the wind through the trees, Molly wasn't sure she'd heard him right. She tried but couldn't pull free, lifted her chin and demanded, in her best Serene Highness voice, "Let me go."

"Happily. Just as soon as we cross the border."

Molly heard that, but didn't hear the helicopter. She didn't even see it until Chase pulled her around and it came soaring over the trees, the same blue and white one they'd seen earlier in the gorge.

It swooped toward them, its skis skimming the tops of the madly pitching evergreens. Only this time, a figure dressed in dark clothes leaned out of the open door on the right side with a gun. A gun pointed right at her head.

20

A BURST of automatic fire exploded the snow at Molly's feet, flung ice in her face and shot her heart up her throat. She whirled to run, just as Chase clamped his arms around her and dove for the trees on the right side of the trail.

Dead branches and grass crusted with ice snapped beneath them. Evergreen boughs lashed at their faces and stole Molly's breath. She was on top when they stopped rolling, but only for the second it took Chase to heave her off him and spring to his knees. She scrambled up beside him, aching and battered, caked with snow and her face stinging, but alive.

She could see the shadow of the chopper hovering just beyond the trees. She saw funnel-shaped clouds of ice and grit swirling up into the rotor. The vibration of the engine made the pine boughs over her head tremble, sprinkled fresh snow down her collar and made her shiver.

With cold, fear and fury. This was her land and her country, God damn it. Shehabi and his thugs had shoved her around and shot at her for the last time.

"That's it," Chase said, breathing deep to catch his breath. "I've had it with these sons of bitches."

Molly couldn't have said it better, so she didn't. Instead she asked, "Why isn't the chopper setting down?"

"If there's somebody coming up the trail behind us, it doesn't have to." Chase wiped blood off a cut on his right cheek with the cold-reddened back of his hand. "All it has to do is keep us pinned here."

"And cut off from the border." Molly gritted her teeth to keep them from chattering. "Unless we do something."

Chase glanced at her over his shoulder as he dug his backpack out of the snow. Where it wasn't red with needle scratches, her face was white with cold, her eyes amber with fury. She had bottom, all right, and then some.

"You bet your crown we're going to do something. I'm gonna distract the chopper and you're gonna get the hell out of here with the Phantom." He opened his backpack and took out a nine millimeter semiautomatic. "I stole this from your father's gun case. It's loaded. Do you know how to use it?"

"Yes." Molly snatched the gun from him, unzipped her jacket and shoved it in the waistband of her jeans. "How are you going to distract the chopper?"

"Ever played chicken?"

"Not with a helicopter."

"Me, either, but I've always wanted to try."

He yanked her bag out from between two rocks and withdrew the scepter. Blood and dirt smeared his cheek and grimed his whiskers, but he was smiling. A grim, dangerous smile that made his eyes flash, like the Phantom atop the scepter, in the gray daylight filtering through the trees.

Molly realized he wasn't kidding, that this wasn't false bravado. He meant it. When he twisted the diamond-studded ruby ring below the crown piece and the Phantom plopped out of its setting into his hand, her mouth fell open.

"How did you know about the lock mechanism?"

"I told you, I know a lot of things."

He was talking to her but staring at the Phantom, his pupils slowly dilating. He'd looked the same way in the Land Rover when she'd thought he was asleep with his eyes open. She knew now that he wasn't, could feel the gears slipping out of place around her again and the slow chill creeping up her back.

Another burst of gunfire ripped past them, slashing through the branches well over their heads and showering them with more snow. Molly flinched and Chase snapped out of his daze. He tucked the scepter under one arm, stuffed the Phantom in her bag, zipped it and grabbed it with the backpack in one hand, Molly's arm in the other and towed her, crouching, a few feet deeper into the trees.

"I'm keeping the scepter," he said, dropping to his knees in the snow in front of her. "Let's hope they want the Phantom more than they want you and they won't notice it's missing. If we're real lucky, they'll be dumb enough to think I'm ditching you and making a break for it."

He opened his backpack, stuffed a package of crackers and an extra clip for the gun into her bag, then swung it over her left shoulder. Molly wanted to wipe the blood off his cheek, but didn't, just bit her lip to keep her chin from quavering and blinked back frightened, angry tears.

"Stay in the trees as much as you can and run like hell for the border. I'll catch up with you."

He didn't say *if I can*. The kiss he clamped on her mouth as he drew her to her feet said it for him. A quick, urgent kiss, shivery with cold and the need to hurry.

"I'll give you a two-minute head start. Don't stop for anything. Just get your butt over the border, find a phone and call Diello."

"Okay," Molly said shakily, though she had no intention of doing it.

She made it look good, though, hiking the strap over her shoulder and scurrying up the ridge. She could still feel Chase's mouth on hers and her heart thumping with the beat of the chopper rotor. She jumped over rocks, wove around trees and low-hanging branches, her knees trembling under the weight of her bag, her breath visible in labored puffs.

She glanced back only once, to make sure Chase was watching the chopper and not her. He was, squinting up at it dipping and tilting from side to side in the wind as it prowled the tree line and he edged toward it about fifty yards behind her. Molly ducked behind a thick-boled pine, swung her bag to the ground and whirled for the trail, bending low and keeping an eye on Chase.

Her cap and jacket blended with the trees. The rattle and hiss of the wind streaming through their crowns masked the crunch of her footsteps through the snow. She reached the trail just as Chase looked at his watch, bit off her gloves and yanked the gun out of her waistband. She checked the clip and flipped off the safety, darted out of the trees and took a spread-footed stance in the middle of the trail, raised the gun in both hands and took careful aim at the blue and white chopper.

The year before he died, her father had sent her and Danny and Otto to a two-week antiterrorist training camp. Molly had graduated first in her class with the highest scores in marksmanship. She knew a 9 mm bullet was powerful enough to shatter bricks; she didn't know if it was powerful enough to bring down a helicopter, but it sure as hell ought to distract one. Drawing and holding a deep breath to steady her aim, she fired two shots.

Chase didn't hear them, but he saw chips of blue paint fly off the chopper's fiberglass hull. He whipped his head around, saw Molly standing in the middle of the trail and the barrel flash three more times.

Sparks flew from the helicopter skis and Chase dove for the ground, gasping a curse at the vicious stab he felt in his left thigh. The ricochet ripped past him into the trees, flinging bark and snow and snapping branches. Chase rolled on his back and dug the open pin of the brooch out of his leg and his pocket. He snapped it shut and tilted his head back. He'd kill Molly for this, if the chopper swinging around to give the gunman a clear shot at her didn't beat him to it.

A sudden, stiff gust of wind caught the chopper in a violent updraft. It reared back on its tail, dipping dangerously close to the ground and knocking the shooter leaning out the open door on Chase's side off balance. He grabbed the frame in both hands, his small, Uzi-size gun swinging free from the strap over his shoulder.

He was dressed in dark clothes with a black ski mask over his face. Behind him, Chase could see the pilot in his seat fighting the stick and the collective. He managed to bring the nose down and level, but it cost him altitude. No more than ten feet off the ground, the chopper hovered steady enough for the gunman to regain his balance and swing the automatic into his hands.

Chase sprang into a run, whipping his head toward Molly and shoving the brooch in his pocket. She was still standing like Clint Eastwood in the middle of the trail. He shouted at her to get down, get out of the way, though he knew she couldn't hear him, and launched himself at the chopper.

The backwash of the rotor nearly flattened him, but he caught the ski with his left hand and hung on, his shoulder wrenching as the chopper fishtailed in the wind. The gunman didn't see him, was too busy fighting to keep his balance.

With his toes dragging the ground, Chase clung to the ski, teeth gritted against the tearing pain in his left arm. When the shooter leaned out of the chopper, foot braced on the ski, he reached up with his right hand, grabbed a fistful of dark pant leg and yanked.

The gunman went sailing over his head, arms outflung. The chopper rocked, the pilot whirled his head, saw Chase and reached for a gun on the control panel. Chase let go of the ski, tucked himself to roll and landed on his right shoulder, the breath whooshing out of him, the chopper lifting and swinging away toward Molly.

The murmur in his head rose to a roar that made his ears ring. Chase pushed up on one elbow and saw the muzzle of the 9 mm in Molly's hands flash twice more. The chopper kept coming, building speed in a nose-down swoop straight at her. She fired two more shots, then spun toward the trees, slipped and fell in a chin-first sprawl on the slick trail.

"Get up, Molly!" Chase jumped to his feet, shouting and running. "God damn it, *get up!*"

Shaking her head woozily, she levered herself up on her hands, just as Chase's left foot shot out from under him on a patch of ice and his left leg wrenched painfully. He grabbed his thigh, felt the hard edges of the brooch beneath his fingers and caught a low-hanging pine branch with his right hand to keep from falling.

The chopper was bearing down on Molly, nose tucked and skis skimming close to the ground. Chase watched her wobble on her knees, turn her head and freeze, her mouth falling open with terror.

"Get down!" he shouted, grabbing tree branches and pulling himself hand-over-hand past the icy patch.

She didn't hear him, didn't move. The chopper closed the gap between them to no more than twenty yards. Chase cleared the ice and started running, limping on his left leg and clutching his thigh, the brooch digging into his palm.

"Veer off, you son of a bitch! *Veer off!*"

The roar in his head crashed like thunder in a vicious gust of nearly gale-force wind that caught the chopper and sent it rolling over on its side, up and away from Molly, spinning tail around and out of control toward the rocky flank of the mountain above the trail. Chase saw Molly blink, scrabble to her feet and throw herself into the trees.

He leapt after her, whirled and watched the chopper heel over in midair, slam into the mountain and explode. The fireball was huge and blinding, but nothing compared to the searing pain in his left thigh. Sucking air between his teeth, he looked down, saw his fingers still clutched over the brooch in his pocket, flung out his hand and saw the imprint of one of the Sanquist lions branded on his palm.

His knees buckled and he went down hard, shoving his hand into the snow. He expected to see steam, but didn't. The heat was suddenly gone, from his palm and his thigh. He pulled his hand out, turned it over and blinked dazedly at his unmarked skin. What the hell?

Chase closed his eyes, opened them and touched his cold, smooth palm. He hadn't imagined the fire or the lion burned into his flesh, but they were gone. There wasn't so much as a blister or a singed spot on his jeans to mark that they'd ever been there.

He drew a shaky breath and tasted gasoline on his tongue, heard the crackle of fire and the crunch of footsteps. He saw Molly running toward him, her face red with cold and exertion, her bag over one shoulder, his backpack over the other, then turned his head and looked at the mountain.

Chunks of burning metal were still falling and hissing onto the trail, melting the snow and raising steam. The tops of the trees on the opposite side were in flames, the wind fanning the fire and the smoke downhill like a giant SOS. They had to get out of here before whoever was climbing up the trail behind them saw it and picked up the pace.

If they hadn't already.

21

THE THOUGHT RACED a warning chill up the back of Chase's neck. He pushed to his feet and walked toward the gunman spread-eagled on his face in the snow, the royal scepter of St. Cristobel on one side of him, his gun half-buried in a drift on the other.

Chase picked up what he'd thought was an Uzi, blew pine needles and snow off it and saw it was a Tec 9, a nasty little Israeli assault rifle. Just the kind of thing Shehabi would keep in stock. Then he picked up the scepter, kicked the gunman over on his back, dropped to his heels and pulled the ski mask off Alec Tremayne's face.

He wasn't surprised. The black garb had tipped him. So had trying to gun them down from a helicopter, a tactic right up Alec's alley. Chase found a pulse beneath his jaw, felt it beating slow but steady, bent his elbows on his knees and looked down at Tremayne's still face.

His eyes were closed, the nasty lump on his forehead already bruising, a trickle of blood in one corner of his mouth. He looked about eighteen. Chase felt about a hundred, the crackling roar of the burning treetops muting the murmur in his head for the first time in twelve hours.

"That's for Jean-Marc," he said.

"I thought Tremayne was dead," Molly said behind him, her voice shaky with cold.

Chase glanced at her over his shoulder, shivering in her snow-soaked jeans and jacket. Her chin was a scraped-up mess, and there were tooth marks on her chapped bottom lip where she'd bitten it when she fell. She bit it again as he stretched to his feet, tucked the scepter in her partially open bag and said, "I thought you were on your way to the border."

Molly hadn't expected gratitude. She hadn't expected anger, either. She wasn't sure what she'd expected, but heat enough to melt a glacier in Chase's eyes wasn't it.

"I happen to be a crack shot," she said defensively.

"Good. Then shoot him." Chase tossed her the Tec 9. "If you don't, he'll just keep dogging us until he gets his hands on the Phantom."

Molly dropped the gun in the snow and skittered away from it, away from him. He didn't like guns; they scared the hell out of him. She remembered that now and understood. Only she didn't.

"If you didn't want me to use it, why did you give me my father's gun?"

"So you could protect yourself if you had to."

"I did."

"How d'you figure that?"

Because I love you, you big jerk, she wanted to scream at him. Instead she said, "Because you have yet to deliver me safely across the border with the Phantom," proving she could be as perverse and obtuse as he was.

"All right, crack shot." Chase pulled the backpack off her left shoulder, her tote off her right and zipped it shut, scooped the Tec 9 out of the snow and shoved it into her hands. "You carry the gun. I'll carry the bags."

"Are you just going to leave him here?" Molly demanded, spinning after him as he started past her.

"Since you don't want to shoot him, yeah." Chase glanced at her, hitching the bags over his shoulders, the grim, dangerous gleam in his eyes again. "Shehabi's thugs will be along to collect him as soon as the fire dies out."

Which wouldn't be long, Molly realized. It was already more smoke than flames, the trees too wet and heavy with snow to burn much. When Alec Tremayne moaned at her feet she started and glanced down at him, saw his forehead crease and one cheek twitch.

Forget being a princess, she wasn't even cut out to be a Savard. Her grandfather had disposed of one hundred and fifty Nazis, Alisander I several hundred of Napoléon's troops. No one knew for sure how many prisoners Prince Sandor had tortured, yet she couldn't even shoot one cowardly little thief. Her father would be so proud of her.

Alec Tremayne had tried to kill her, and would again if he caught up with them. Molly knew that, found the safety on the gun, flipped it and looped it over her shoulder by its webbed strap. She couldn't shoot him, but she could put as much distance between them as fast as she could.

Which was obviously what Chase intended, striding ahead of her triple time. Molly ran to catch up, coughing and batting at the oil smoke drifting across the trail and dodging smoldering bits of the helicopter. She figured he was trying to get even with her, an impulse as childish and silly as hers to keep up with him, even if it killed her.

He didn't stop, didn't so much as slow down until they reached the top of the ridge and the mountain road marking the border between St. Cristobel and France. By the time Molly swung her right leg over the guardrail and dropped onto it, hard enough to shoot a twinge of pain up her tailbone, spots were dancing before her eyes, her legs were shuddering and her arms shaking.

She was done for, finished, exhausted. Chase realized it when he turned and saw her straddling the rail, her shoulders and her head bowed, the Tec 9 slipping by its strap down her right arm.

The road ran between two mountains, the one on his left in St. Cristobel, the one on his right in France. The wind howled through the two-lane-wide gap between them, shredding the remnants of the storm clouds high overhead. It whistled in his ears, overriding the incessant, nerve-rattling murmur in his head, and set his teeth on edge. He wished to hell it would stop—and it did.

The sun came out and a slow, crawling chill slithered up Chase's back. His left hand shook as he dragged it through his snarled hair and looked at his palm. No burns or blisters, but he'd wished it and the wind had stopped. For the first time in his life, he wanted desperately to believe in coincidence.

He forced himself to shake off the chill and concentrate on the pale glimmer of green he could just see beyond the curve looping around the French peak. The few indistinguishable lumps he hoped were a village. It was hard to tell how far away they were, but he figured at least six or seven miles. Molly couldn't quit on him. Not yet.

He took the thermos out of the backpack, walked to her, filled the cap and handed it to her. She emptied it in two gulps and held it out for a refill. He gave it to her, took a slug from the thermos, fished his shades out of the backpack, put them on and scanned the ridge.

The trail was empty, the snowy slope blinding in the sun. A thin wisp of smoke, either from the burning trees or the wreck of the chopper, still drifted toward the *schloss*. The crawl up his back had eased some, but not the murmur in his head. He was beginning to wonder if he'd cracked his head on the mantel hard enough to concuss himself.

At least it was a logical explanation. He refused to think about the illogical, the frightening possibility that the Sanquist curse existed, that it was as real as the lion he'd seen burned on his palm.

"We better get a move on," he said, taking the cap and screwing it on the thermos.

"Gimme a minute," Molly murmured wearily.

"We don't have a minute." Chase tucked the thermos in the backpack and looked down his nose at her over his sunglasses. "We're barely one jump ahead of them as it is."

Her chin shot up and she glared at him. "Would you prefer that I faint and you have to carry me?"

"I won't carry you. I'll drag you."

"The hell you will." She pushed herself up and off the rail, stumbling as she swung her left leg over it.

Chase braced himself to catch her, but she didn't fall. The Tec 9 did, with a clatter onto the ice-edged pavement. She didn't pick it up, just gave it a savage sideways kick that sent it sailing under the guardrail and skittering down the rocky slope.

"I'm not going to shoot anybody," she said between gritted teeth, and struck off shakily down the side of the road.

Chase tried to take her arm but she shrugged his hand away and snapped, "Keep your hands off me."

"Fine, Highness. Just remember if you faint I'll have to drag you."

"I'll crawl first." She turned toward him on one foot, her fatigue-smudged eyes blazing amber. "I'll drag *myself*, by God, by my fingernails if I have to."

"Suit yourself." Chase shrugged the bags higher on his shoulders and started walking, keeping to the French side of the double yellow line down the middle of the road, turning his head just enough so he could watch her out of the corner of his eye. She drew a deep breath and followed him in small, mincing steps. "Do your feet hurt?"

"Not anymore. Now they're numb."

Chase stopped about ten yards ahead of her and turned. "Sounds like frostbite," he said, crossing the yellow line into St. Cristobel.

"No kidding," she snapped, easing herself onto the guardrail with her weight braced on the heels of her hands.

Bars of cold, vivid light and deep shadow slanted across the granite flank of the mountain behind her. Icicles dripped about twenty feet above her, from a ledge piled with several feet of scallop-edged snow. It would have been a picture to cherish in memory, except for the scowl on Molly's face.

"Don't bitch at me, Your Highness." Chase dropped to his heels in front of her, swung the bags off his shoulders and opened her tote. "I can't control the weather."

"This from the man who wished it would snow and it did."

"That was a fluke." Chase bent his head and rummaged in her bag for a pair of socks. For a second, all he saw was the blinding blue-white brilliance of the Phantom half-buried in her rumpled clothes. He felt his jaw slacken, the murmur in his head swell, but shook it off, dug out a pair of white ribbed anklets and tossed them up to her. "Put these on."

"I don't think the snow was a fluke. I think it was weird." Molly bent her right foot on her left knee and untied her frozen black laces. "If I didn't know better, I'd think it was the curse on the Phantom. It's supposed to give anybody named Sanquist who touches it everything his heart desires, you know."

A jolt of surprise shot through Chase. "How d'you know about the curse?"

She pried off her shoe and dropped it with a soggy thunk and an arch smile. "I know a lot about a lot of things."

"You sound like Achmed." Chase closed her bag with a quick rip of the zipper. The murmur in his head dropped a decibel, but his thigh, where the brooch had stabbed him, began to throb like a toothache. "Or worse yet, Shehabi."

"I take it you don't believe the curse," she said, peeling off her sock. It was soaked and black in places where the dye had rubbed off her shoes. So was her foot, where it wasn't red with cold and white with frostbite.

"Hell, no, I don't believe it." Chase shut and buckled the flap of the backpack. "Hurry up, will you?"

"Then how," she asked, pulling on a dry sock, "do you explain the fact that it snowed when you wished it?"

"I did explain it. I said it was a fluke."

"But what if it wasn't?"

"Drop it, Princess." Chase flung the bags over his shoulders and pushed to his feet. "Get your socks changed and let's go."

"Ooh, hit a nerve." She put on her right shoe, took off her left one and her sock. "You're awful touchy for a man who doesn't believe in curses."

"I'm just the right amount of touchy," Chase growled, "for a man with every thug in St. Cristobel on his tail."

"Why don't you just *wish* them off your tail? Or better yet—" she raised her foot and waggled her cold-whitened toes at him, her eyes gleaming with mischief and malice "—why don't you wish my sock and my shoe on my foot?"

She was angry and hurt and trying to hurt him back. Chase knew that, but it didn't help. He was losing patience with her—and his temper. The warning chill was creeping up his neck again. He wanted out of here, off this high, open road under a calm and sunny sky. Where there was one helicopter, there was apt to be another.

"I'll go you one better," he said. "Why don't I just wish you'd shut up?"

"Go ahead." She leaned forward on her hands, her mouth urved in a taunting smile. "Wish me to shut up."

"Don't tempt me." Chase moved away from her, away om the bulk of the mountain, and squinted up at the sky. Ie saw only a pair of kites gliding high above the moun-ains, but that didn't mean there wasn't something else fly-ıg around up there, on rotors rather than wings.

"Don't worry," she said sourly. "I've been trying."

"Knock it off, Princess." Chase rounded on her, his heart nd the murmur in his head pounding, flashes of blue-white ght pulsing on the edges of his vision. "We don't have time or games."

"Do you know your eyes glaze over when you look at the hantom?" She leaned back on her hands and cocked her ead at him. "It's like you drift off into a daze or some-ning. It's absolutely the weirdest thing I've ever—"

"*Shut up!*" Chase shouted, his voice bouncing back at im off the soaring flanks of the mountains. "Shut your 10uth or I'll shut it for you!"

She blinked at him, startled, then said sweetly, "That's ll I want."

"If it'll get you up and moving, then fine," Chase gritted etween clenched teeth. "I wish to hell you'd shut up."

She gave it a five count, then an exaggerated sigh and bent er foot across her knee. "Gee, sorry. Guess it doesn't vork." She tugged on her sock, then her shoe and tied it. Guess you'll just have to listen to me bitch."

An icicle broke loose from the ledge above her, a big one, bout six feet long and as thick as Chase's arm. It plum-neted like a spear to the ground and shattered like glass, xploding shards of ice across the road. If Molly hadn't tood up and stepped away from the guardrail, it would ave hit her square on the head—and definitely would have hut her up. Maybe permanently.

Chase knew it, and so did Molly. The sudden, sick clutch
in his gut and the wide-eyed look she flung up at the snow-
packed ledge above her told him so—half a second before
a second icicle snapped like a gunshot, tore loose from the
ledge and fractured the thin sheaf of ice holding the six or
so feet of snow above her head in place.

It all came down on top of her, in a boiling, roiling white
cloud that buried the guardrail, half the roadway and the
Princess Royal of St. Cristobel.

22

CHASE RIPPED OFF the bags and Prince Alisander's jacket and leapt into the avalanche before it stopped moving. He ignored the snow that was still shifting and hissing around him and started digging frantically to find Molly.

Within seconds his bare hands were burning. So was the brooch in his pocket, with heat, not cold. Just like it had when the chopper had slammed into the mountain. The realization made his skin crawl. He dropped to his knees, scooping snow with his right hand, digging the brooch out of his pocket with his left and tossing it away.

It landed hissing and steaming in the snow, melted a couple of inches and exposed the ribbed green cuff of Molly's jacket. Chase didn't think, just grabbed it and used it like a laser to burn the snow off her, the murmur in his head crashing like thunder, his mind screaming at him that this was impossible, *impossible*.

But it worked. He had Molly free in seconds, limp and soaked, the corners of her mouth faintly tinged with blue. He tore off her jacket and her cap, undid her jeans and started CPR. Between reps he paused to suck a breath and saw the brooch snagged on the shoulder of her sweater.

"Give her back, you son of a bitch," he cursed it. "You took her, you goddamn *give her back!*"

His voice echoed back at him, ragged with panic, and then she breathed. Once, a shuddery, shallow breath that ended in a paroxysm of coughing and gagging. Chase rolled her over, cradled her head in one hand, her stomach in the

other and let her heave. Gasping and choking, but breathing. Alive and breathing.

Chase thanked God, not the brooch, but let go of Molly
long enough to work it free of her sweater and shove it in
his pocket. He held her in his hands again as another round
of dry heaves seized her, raised his head and swallowed hard
when his gag reflex threatened to trigger.

His gaze fell on her tote bag where he'd dropped it on the
road. It was pulsing, a dim, murky blue, in perfect time with
his thudding heartbeat.

Every hair on his body stood on end, prayers he hadn't
said in years racing through his head. He closed his eyes and
clung to the prayers, clung to Molly, lifting her into his arms
to warm her. Her body was convulsed with shivers, and she
was only semiconscious. Her skin was so pale he could see
the tiny blue veins in her eyelids above her fluttering lashes.

Chase prayed for sanity, and an ambulance with a team
of paramedics. He got a truck, an old beige Citroën pickup
with rusty fenders and a bad muffler but excellent brakes.

The driver had a thin dark mustache and a billed tweed
cap on his head. He jumped out of the cab, running and
calling, "What happened? Is madame hurt?" In lilting, thick
country French, not the oddly accented, German-influenced
dialect spoken in St. Cristobel.

Chase pushed to his feet with Molly in his arms, ad-
libbing a version of the truth that made her his wife and put
them on holiday, out hiking when the sudden storm over-
took them and a ledge full of snow collapsed on her. Monsieur Bouvard introduced himself and helped Chase climb
into the cab with her.

Then he tossed their bags into the truck bed, jumped behind the wheel and let off the brake. The old Citroën shot
like a bullet into the curve bound for France, tires squeal-

ing, Chase tightening his arms around Molly's shivering body.

Freak storms were common in the mountains this time of year. Monsieur Bouvard could not imagine the concierge of Deux-Montagnes, the ski lodge but a few miles from where he'd found them, not warning them of the danger.

Such a thing was not done at Chez Bouvard, the small but excellent inn he and his wife ran in the village of Solange, for which they were bound at nearly fifty miles an hour, through twists and turns that would have tried even Chase's driving skills. He didn't correct the assumption, just made a noncommittal noise in his throat and cupped a hand around Molly's face. Her skin felt like ice, clammy ice.

"Do not worry, Monsieur—"

"Sanquist," Chase said. If Bouvard asked for ID, it had better match whatever he said.

"Do not worry, Monsieur Sanquist. Madame is only cold and a little in shock, perhaps. We have no doctor, but we have my Sophie. She will know what to do."

She knew to come running when Monsieur Bouvard laid on the horn as he careened the truck into the cobbled inn yard, through an open gate in a whitewashed wall. Madame Bouvard, too, had a mustache, but a round, gentle face that clouded with concern when her husband stopped the truck, leapt out of it and told her what had happened.

"Fetch the brandy, Maurice," she said, holding the inn door open for Chase. "Up the stairs, monsieur, the last door on your left. Do not worry, madame will be fine."

Chase wished to God they'd stop telling him that. He bounded up the steps with Molly, his arms shuddering by the time he laid her on a feather bed in the room on the right at the end of the hall. Madame told her husband to draw a bath and took white terry-cloth bath sheets from an armoire on one wall. While Chase stripped Molly out of her filthy, ice-caked clothes, madame worked behind him wrapping her in the big towels.

She looked like a mummy by the time they finished and he carried her into the adjoining bathroom. A moan escaped her lips and her teeth began to chatter when Chase went down on his knees beside the tub and eased her into the tepid water.

"We must bring the blood back slowly," madame said.

It took three tubs of lukewarm water to leach the deathly gray pallor from Molly's face. The muscles in Chase's lower back were screaming, but his throat swelled and ached with relief as he watched a faint pink flush wash her cheeks and her eyes flutter slowly open.

"Hi, there," he said gently. "Welcome back."

She smiled weakly, blinking like an owl between the folds of wet towel draped around her head and shoulders. "Where are we?" she asked, her voice sounding thick and sleepy.

"In France. In an inn. This is Madame Bouvard." Chase leaned back on his heels so Molly could see her.

She smiled at Molly and nodded. "*Bonsoir, madame.* How do you feel?"

Good evening? Chase glanced at the small window above the tub. The bright blue sky was fading and faintly tinged with purple and mauve. Jesus. No wonder his back hurt.

"I'm fine. I think." Molly sat up slowly, stiffly, sloshing water and clutching the folds of the towels around her. "I don't remember—" Her breath caught and her eyes widened. "Oh, yes, I do. Oh, God. I remember—"

"You're okay, Princess." Chase sprang up on his knees and wrapped his arms around her. "You're fine. Just fine. Think about that."

Don't remember that I damn near killed you. I didn't mean to, but I— Wait a minute. He hadn't damn near killed her. The Phantom had. At last, Chase understood the murmur in his head and felt his blood run cold.

Molly leaned the back of her towel-wrapped head against his shoulder and peered at him. "You look like hell," she said, a rusty edge in her voice.

Madame Bouvard laughed, pushed to her feet and sat on the lid of the toilet to wipe her hands on her white apron. Chased turned on his knees, caught her right hand and kissed it ardently.

"And now the brandy," Monsieur Bouvard said, stepping into the bathroom with a squat brown bottle and four glasses on a little tray. He put it on the sink, uncorked the bottle and filled the glasses, bowing to Molly as he passed hers to Chase and murmured, "*Enchanté, Madame Sanquist.*"

Molly's hand caught as she reached out of her towels to take the glass. Her lips parted, and Chase kissed them, whispering in her ear, "I had to tell him something."

"Come, Maurice." Madame Bouvard rose, the corners of her mouth curled in an *ah, l'amour* smile directed at Molly. "You may take off the towels now and draw a fresh bath. I will bring a basket for the wet things, monsieur."

"Will you be okay alone?" Chase got to his feet, one hand on the shower curtain. "I want to clean up."

Molly nodded. He drew the curtain and followed the Bouvards out of the bathroom. "Madame, if you please," he said, "I need a couple things from your kitchen—"

The door closed, and that's all Molly heard. Like what? she wondered, but couldn't work up much curiosity. Her brain felt sluggish and her bones like sponge, but she managed to drain the tub, wring the towels and toss them in the sink. Then she filled the tub with stingingly warm water, added bubble bath from a plastic bottle on the side, leaned back with a sigh and shut her eyes.

There was a dull, thudding ring in her ears and her in
sides were still quivering. Her bottom lip did, too, when a
picture of the snow ledge breaking loose flashed through her
head. She bit her lip, hard, and opened her eyes, the bub
bles foaming around her blurring with tears.

She didn't want to cry, but she couldn't stop. It was
physical shock and emotional reaction to everything that
had happened since Chase had kissed her hand in the re
ceiving line. Her palace had been bombed and burned, she'd
been chased by her own guards, shot at from a helicopter
and buried alive. Oh, yeah. And she'd fallen in love with a
thief.

What a night. What a guy. Chase wanted her diamond
but he didn't want her. Molly turned off the water, spread
a washcloth over her raised knees, buried her face in it and
wept.

23

THE FIRST THING Chase did was make sure the Bouvards hadn't recognized the princess. He didn't think so, since the filthy, half-frozen girl in their best guest room bore about as much resemblance to the one who routinely graced the cover of *Paris Match* as he did to Alec Tremayne.

The second thing he did was down four brandies with monsieur. Then he took a shower, washed his hair and shaved in madame's second-best guest room. His hands shook so badly it was a miracle he didn't cut his throat.

The third thing he did was have two more brandies. Then he borrowed a box of salt and a box of baking soda and headed upstairs in a blue terry-cloth robe borrowed from monsieur with one made of pink chenille loaned by madame for the princess over his arm.

He heard her crying in the bathroom five feet shy of the guest room. He heard the Phantom calling to him from the black nylon bag Monsieur Bouvard had brought in from the truck along with the backpack. He locked the door behind him and did his damnedest not to think about anything.

The Phantom didn't like that; its murmur turned petulant. Goddamn stone was probably female. Chase wished he'd kept the brandy and lighted a cigarette from the pack Monsieur Bouvard had given him. Booze had a better kick, but the nicotine rush played havoc with his head, made it trickier for the Phantom to tune in to him.

He carried his cigarette to the window and drew the lace curtain aside. Beyond the wall enclosing the inn, a flagged patio and madame's garden, the fields surrounding the village stretched all the way to distant purple and charcoal foothills on the storm-smudged horizon.

Thunder rumbled, low and far away. Wonderful. It was going to rain again. Chase let the curtain fall and lighted another cigarette. The Phantom grumbled. He'd realized in the shower that the stone couldn't think, that it could only reflect the thoughts and energies it absorbed from him, the same way it absorbed heat and light.

The kicker was it intensified them, and magnified the emotions that accompanied them a thousandfold. He had no idea how, he only knew from recreating the chopper crash and the ledge coming down on Molly, the temper fit he'd thrown in Jean-Marc's shop and in the village square, that it did.

He'd figured out while he shaved that the Phantom had a literal mind. It was only concerned with the end—giving him what he wanted—not the means. The crash had killed a man, and Molly had damn near been buried alive, but the chopper had veered off and she'd definitely shut up.

The princess was still crying, but he couldn't wait. Not if he wanted to give her what she wanted without interference. He put out his cigarette and turned down the bed, picked up madame's robe, the salt and baking soda and the black nylon bag. He'd put the brooch in the pocket of monsieur's robe after his shower, but he wasn't going to touch the Phantom until he had to.

"Princess?" Chase knocked on the bathroom door. "May I come in?"

Water sloshed and the rings holding the shower curtain on the metal rod shrieked. Chase heard her choke back tears and the quaver in her voice when she said, "If you must."

He shut the door quickly behind him so he wouldn't make a draft and hung madame's robe over the towel bar. Molly's silhouette on the curtain slid lower in the tub.

"Sorry to barge in." He put the bag on the toilet and plugged the sink. "But I can't do this anyplace else."

Chase filled the sink and opened the salt and the baking soda. He couldn't remember how much to use, and of course he'd lost Jean-Marc's recipe. He dumped half a box of each in the water, swished it around, dropped the brooch in the sink, picked up the bag and unzipped it.

The Phantom raised its voice and the murmur in his head joyfully. He gritted his teeth and picked up the stone, his skin crawling as it began to glow in his hand and pulse along with his heartbeat. Chase wanted to drop it but didn't, just eased it into the sink and backed away, rubbing his wet hand on monsieur's robe.

The murmur in his head took on a watery gurgle. The Phantom glimmered at him, its facets wavering and undulating beneath the surface of water. He dumped more salt and more soda into the sink.

"What are you doing?" the princess asked.

In the corner of the steam-fogged mirror above the sink, Chase saw her peering at him around the drawn-back edge of the shower curtain. She had a towel wrapped around her head, a fresh-scrubbed glow on her face and bubbles floating provocatively around her bare, shapely shoulders.

"I'm cleansing the Phantom," he told her. "The brooch, too, I hope to God."

She tipped her head curiously to one side and bent her elbow on the edge of the tub. "How'd they get dirty?"

"Contaminated is a better word," he said.

The murmur in his head was fading. Not gone, but fading. Chase figured he wouldn't be able to get rid of it completely until he found a way to break the stone's hold on him. And how in hell he was going to do that he had no idea. Not yet.

"Or maybe corrupted," he added, sitting down on the toilet seat to talk to the princess.

"You mean the curse," she said.

"I can't believe it, but yes, I mean the curse."

He leaned forward and bent his elbows on his knees. The bathroom was small enough that it brought his face within half a foot of hers. She didn't close the curtain or draw away, but a pulse leapt in the damp hollow of her throat.

"I didn't mean to hurt you, Princess. I'm sorry."

"I'm sorry I goaded you into it."

"It wasn't your fault."

"It wasn't yours, either. It was the Phantom."

"Listen to us." Chase shook his head and ran a hand through his half-dry hair. "We're talking about a lump of carbon like it's alive."

"Maybe it is," Molly suggested. "Just not alive like we think of it."

"Maybe, though that's not what Jean-Marc said. He said diamonds absorb thoughts and actions as well as energy." Chase let his hand fall and his gaze drift past the column of her throat to the shadow of her breasts below the bubbles bobbing on the water. "Particularly psychic energy."

"Yech." She disappeared behind the curtain, sinking lower in the tub. "Prince Sandor alone is enough to foul a stone the size of the Phantom," she said, her voice sounding hollow. "But if you throw in Shehabi's ancestor and a couple other Savards I can think of—"

"Don't forget the Sanquists," Chase put in. "We had the stone for a good long time."

She pushed herself up, sloshing water and pulling the curtain back. "How many murderers and torturers on your family tree?"

"Only a couple," he said with a wry smile. "The Sanquists run more to drink and debauchery."

She smiled and leaned her head against the tub. Thunder rumbled and the lights flickered. So did her eyes.

"And thieving," she said. "Don't forget that."

"Don't you forget it, either," Chase warned her.

"Oh, raspberries on you, Sanquist." She scooped up a handful of bubbles and flicked them at him. "You're no more a big bad thief than I am. If you were, you would have taken off with the Phantom and left me buried alive on the side of the road for the kites to pick my bones when the snow melts."

She lifted her chin, daring him to deny it. Her bubbles were rapidly dissipating. He could see the lush, shadowy curve of her hips beneath the water. He could see where she was going with this, too, and followed along.

"For your information, Princess, I wouldn't have left Alec Tremayne buried alive on the side of the road."

"So why are you still here? You saved my life, I'm obviously all right. I've been in here long enough to turn myself into a prune—" she held up her wrinkled right hand as proof "—but you're still here. Why haven't you stolen me blind and split?"

"Is that why you were crying? Because you thought I was going to steal your jewels and leave you?"

She didn't answer, just glared at him and raked the curtain shut. Chase dropped to his knees and opened it. She turned her head and looked at him, shivering with gooseflesh, her arms wrapped around her drawn-up knees.

"Or were you crying," he asked gently, "because you were afraid I wouldn't?"

"I don't know." She leaned her chin on her knees and stared at the taps. "Maybe both, maybe neither. I'm so tired and so confused I don't know what I want."

"Do you want to make love?" Chase asked, spreading his hands on the wet edge of the tub.

Her head whipped toward him, so quickly one end of the towel came untucked from her turban.

"I thought," she said flatly, "you wanted to have sex."

"I changed my mind." Chase leaned into the tub and kissed her, tipping up her head and her chin so he could cup her cheek and trace the line of her jaw with his thumb.

He felt her moan and her mouth tremble. When her lips parted, he grazed his tongue across her teeth, pulled back and looked at her. Her eyes were shining.

"I want to make love to you, Princess."

"My name," she said pointedly, "is Molly."

"I know your name." He pulled off her towel, threaded his fingers into her hair and cupped her head in his hands. "I'm saving it for just the right moment."

"When's that?" she asked, lifting her eyes to his face.

"Come to bed with me," Chase murmured against her mouth, "and find out."

She shivered and parted her lips. So did Chase, letting his tongue slip into her mouth, shifting his hands to cradle her face. When she moaned again, he felt it all the way down his throat, felt her knees slide into the water. He sucked gently at her mouth, moved his hands to cup her shoulders and rolled her up on her knees.

Her hands found the belt of monsieur's robe and fumbled the knot out of it. When he slipped his arms around her and drew her to her feet, backing up so she could step out of the tub, she slid her hands inside the robe and pressed her body against his. He was perfectly in control until then, until he felt her breasts and her hips against his. Cool, wet and so hot he had to break the kiss and suck a steadying breath.

She lifted her lashes and looked at him, her eyes shimmering, locked her left hand over her right wrist and grazed her fingernails across the small of his back. When he groaned, she smiled.

"On second thought," he said raggedly, "maybe we should just have sex. Hot and quick. Right here. Right now."

"After you call me Molly," she said, stretching up on her toes to kiss his chin.

He caught her mouth in his and scooped her up in his arms. She tucked her head in the curve of his neck and kept it there until he laid her on the bed. When she stretched out her arms and felt the sheets, she arched an eyebrow at him and said, "You planned this."

For a second he couldn't speak. He could only stare at her shining eyes, tousled, gold-streaked hair and the pale, wet gleam of her lushly slim body in the storm-darkened sunset filtering through madame's lace curtains.

"Every step of the way."

"Good." She smiled and opened her arms.

Chase stripped off monsieur's robe and braced himself above her on his hands. "I think," he said, letting his gaze drift over her, "that I'm looking at the real riches of St. Cristobel."

"You're a wonderful liar." She laughed, twining her arms around his neck.

"I'm telling the truth, Princess." Chase cupped his right hand around her left breast, lowered his head and kissed her nipple. It peaked against his tongue. So did her right breast when he kissed it. "You're absolutely gorgeous," he murmured, raising his head to kiss her parted lips.

She slid her tongue under his, her hands across his shoulders, down his arms and splayed her fingers on his chest. She found his nipples with her nails and teased them. Chase nipped at her tongue, her lower lip, then raised his head and smiled at her. She smiled at him, her eyes a soft, misty green.

"That drives me crazy," he told her softly, "and I'd love to let you do it all night long, but we can't stay here. You know that, don't you?"

"Yes," she said, dropping her gaze.

"I'll make it up to you." He lifted her hands from his chest and wrapped them around his neck. "Kiss me, Molly."

She smiled, parted her lips and pulled his mouth over hers just as the rain began a soft, slow patter against the window. Chase slid his arms beneath her, cupped her head in his hands and let himself sink on top of her, his weight on his knees. She laced her fingers into his hair, broke the kiss and opened her eyes.

"Where are we going?"

"Glyco," Chase decided, as he nuzzled her collarbone.

He felt her stiffen beneath him and raised his head. Her eyes weren't soft anymore, and neither was the rain. It pelted the windows, hard and cold as her eyes.

"Glyco is what I am, it's the reason I'm a thief. I want you to see it. I want you to understand."

Her eyes softened and she touched his chin, let the tip of her index finger trace his lower lip. "You're an incredible liar, Sanquist."

"Wait'll you meet my uncle Cosmo."

She tipped her head back on the pillow and laughed until Chase buried his lips in the hollow of her throat. She gasped then, when he swirled his tongue, and opened her legs. Chase went up on his elbows and nudged her. She was hot, wet, and oh, so soft. He kissed her and drove into her. She moaned and arched her hips, tried to push him up on his knees and drive against him.

He wouldn't let her. He took her tongue in his mouth and suckled, stroked her, slow and soft, until she gasped and moaned and shuddered, raked his shoulders, clutched his hair and went limp underneath him with a whimper. He held her, rubbing his lips across her damp hairline until she sighed, "Oh, Chase."

"Ever been kissed to sleep?" he asked, nuzzling her ear.

"No."

"Wanna be?"

"Oh, yes."

It didn't take long. He knew it wouldn't. She was exhausted. She went to sleep with a smile on her face, her cheeks flushed and her mouth swollen.

He had a lot to do, but he took time to watch her sleep, to tuck the covers around her and cup her breasts, so softly she didn't stir, time to savor her and remember what it was like to be with someone who loved him.

Someone he could love if he let himself.

24

MOLLY EXPECTED CHASE to be gone when she woke up. She
expected it to be morning, too, as exhausted as she was, but
it was still dark when her eyes sprang open, and Chase was
still with her.

Not beside her in bed, but in the upholstered armchair in
front of the tiled fireplace. He'd lighted a cigarette and a fire
and sat sideways in the chair with his plaid thrown over his
bare shoulders staring into the flames.

A log snapped and broke, shooting sparks up the chim-
ney. The fire danced on the glass screen standing ajar so he
could flick his ash into the hearth, cast silver shadows on
his tousled hair and gleamed on the long, muscled length of
his right leg hooked over the arm of the chair.

He looked so handsome Molly's throat ached. So did her
sore arms as she tossed her pillow to the foot of the bed, and
the muscles in her calves as she crawled on top of it, shivered in the damp chill in the room and drew the spread over
her.

"I didn't know you smoked," she said, bending her elbow and propping her chin on her hand.

"I don't." Chase turned his head and smiled at her, smoke
drifting from his nostrils. "But the nicotine messes up my
mind just enough to keep the Phantom off balance."

He told her about the murmur in his head and felt himself stir looking at her wrapped in white chenille. The glow
from the fire barely reached the bed, tipping her hair silver

where it tangled over one shoulder, shadowing the frown that crept across her forehead as she listened to him.

"How do you stand it?" She rocked back on her heels and wound the spread around her like a toga. "I'd go nuts."

"I have phenomenal self-control, even if I do say so myself," he said, taking a drag on his cigarette. "Most of the time, anyway."

He lighted another one as Molly scooted across the cold hardwood floor between the bed and the hooked rug by the fire. He smiled and threw the cigarette away when she knelt at his feet, brushed his knuckles across her cheek as she laced her fingers over his left knee and leaned her chin on them.

"You haven't slept, have you?"

"I've been watching you. That's almost as good."

He didn't tell her he was afraid to sleep, that he'd nodded off once and jerked awake with the murmur in his head going strong again. He'd packed all their stuff so they could leave as soon as Molly woke up. He'd unpacked it in a hurry. The stone and the brooch were soaking in the sink again in the last of madame's salt and baking soda.

Molly unlaced her fingers and laid her cheek against his knee, felt the warmth in his skin and the hard muscle underneath it. She closed her eyes and savored the gentle stroke of his fingers against her temple.

"I thought you'd be gone when I woke up."

"Princess, Princess," he said with a sigh, letting his fingertips trail down her throat. "I couldn't leave you now if I wanted to."

Liar, Molly thought, but turned her head and softly rubbed her lips against the inside of his knee. He made a noise in his throat, part moan but mostly growl. She nuzzled a path up his thigh, raised her head and looked at him.

She wanted him again. Chase saw it in the firelight gleaming in her eyes, in the curve of her shoulder and the swell of her breasts above the bedspread wrapped around her. A chill brushed up his back but he ignored it, slid his fingers through her hair and cupped her face.

"Go ahead," he murmured. "I love it."

She kissed his palm, stretched her arms around his waist and bent over him. He spread her hair in his hands, watched the long strands gleam red and gold in his fingers. When her mouth brushed him, softly, tentatively, he closed his eyes and tipped his head back against the chair. The murmur in his head swelled, but he forced it back, pushed it away. If he was going to go crazy, he'd let the princess drive him there.

She damn near did. When she lifted her head, her eyes were soft and shining, and he was breathless and throbbing. His fingers were still threaded in her hair, her face cupped in his hands. When he traced her lower lip with his thumb, she caught in her teeth and sucked.

The noise Chase made in his throat shot a thrill through Molly. He might not love her, but he wanted her. She saw it in his heavy, half-lidded eyes, felt it in the tremble of his fingers as he loosed her hair and the spread wrapped around her. She arched her back, let her breasts spill into his hands and caught his wrists to hold them there.

"Oh, Princess," he sighed, with a sharp intake of breath.

"My name," she said, rubbing softly against him, "is Molly."

"Your name," he growled, lifting his plaid off his shoulders and looping it around hers, "is Marie-Marguerite Christiana Alistrina Helene Savard. Princess Royal of St. Cristobel and love of my life."

He tugged her into his lap, spread her legs over him and slid inside her, hard and hot enough to make her shiver and clamp herself around him. He kissed her throat and gripped her hips, thrusting and rocking her on top of him.

Molly twined her arms around his neck, her fingers in his hair. She pressed her cheek against his temple, clung to him and loved him so fiercely tears sprang behind her closed eyes. Her pulse throbbed against his mouth, and his breath shot hot shivers across her breasts. When he caught her nipple in his teeth the shivers coursed through her in lush, shuddering waves that left her limp and whimpering, her lips shivering against his forehead.

"Molly, sweet." He kissed her shoulder and wrapped his plaid around her. "We have to go."

"Now?" She leaned her head back and blinked at him, startled. She could feel him still throbbing inside of her. "Aren't you going to, um, finish?"

"Much as I'd love to, no." He caught her hips and eased her gently away from him. "Natalie would never forgive me if I sent you home pregnant."

Molly felt her face flame. She hadn't thought of that. Still she tossed her hair defiantly over one shoulder and notched up her chin. "It's *my* body."

"But it's *my* choice," he said gently, tracing her lower lip with his thumb.

Molly wanted to bite it off but didn't, just gathered his plaid and her dignity and slid off his lap. She should be glad and grateful, but she wasn't. She was hurt and angry and humiliated. She wanted to cry, but snatched up her bag, fled into the bathroom and locked the door.

The tears in her eyes froze and she sat down, hard, shivering on the edge of the bathtub when she turned on the light and saw the Phantom and the brooch soaking in the sink. She remembered what Chase told her about the murmur in his head and felt silly and ashamed.

Somehow the Phantom had gotten inside of him, was driving him crazy—no matter what he said—and she was acting like a spoiled, petulant child. High damn time she started acting like a princess.

Using the bathtub tap, she washed quickly and put on jeans and socks, a lavender turtleneck and a gold and lavender splash-printed sweater. It clashed horribly, but she wrapped Chase's plaid around her shoulders anyway and put on her mostly dry Reeboks.

Molly brushed her hair, tugged a towel off the bar and took the Phantom and the brooch out of the sink. She wiped them off, put them in her bag and swung it over her shoulder as she opened the door.

The bedside lamp was on, the low-watt bulb casting long shadows on the rumpled sheets. Chase was on his knees, dousing the fire and closing the screen. He glanced at her over his shoulder, already dressed in jeans and a cream-colored Aryan knit sweater.

"Stay there," she said, flipping off the light.

"What for?"

"Just a second." Molly put the bag down, well away from him, took out the royal scepter and walked up to him. "I usually do this with Prince Sandor's sword, but since you're a Sanquist, it's probably just as well the damn thing's in St. Cristobel. I can fake it with the scepter."

"Fake what?" Chase asked, one eyebrow sliding up.

"For service to the Crown of St. Cristobel," Molly said solemnly, grasping the scepter in both hands, "particularly to the person of Her Serene Highness Marie-Marguerite, we bestow upon Chastain Sanquist of Glyco, Scotland, the title Count of San Blanco. With our undying gratitude and Almighty God as our witness."

She held her breath and touched the empty crown piece to his right shoulder, afraid to look at him, afraid he'd shrug it off. He didn't, just stayed very still on his knees until she touched the scepter to his left shoulder, then he bowed his head and shook it slowly.

Uh-oh. Bad idea, Molly thought, stepping quickly away from him. "I can take it back if you want."

"No, Princess. I'm honored, truly." He raised his head and looked at her, his eyebrow sliding higher and devilment twinkling in his sapphire eyes. "I was just wondering exactly how you define service to the person of Her Serene Highness."

"I won't, not *exactly*," she replied, laughing with relief. "Not on the proclamation, anyway."

"Thank you." He caught her wrists and stood up, wrapped her arms around his waist and planted a slow, soft kiss on her mouth. "Especially for not using a sword. I'm a little skittish around Savards with swords in their hand."

"You are most welcome." Molly gave him a royal nod. "I also put the Phantom and the brooch in my bag."

"Thank you," he repeated, pressing a fervent kiss between her eyebrows. "Ready?"

"Are we sneaking out like thieves in the night?" Molly asked. "You'll forgive the expression."

"A good thief doesn't have to sneak, Highness." Chase pulled a single key on a slim ring from his pocket. "I paid Monsieur Bouvard handsomely for the loan of his truck and three nights' lodging while you slept."

"Wait a minute." Molly turned away from him. "I'd like to leave something for madame."

"I already did," Chase said, as she swung her bag off the floor and opened it. "The blue topaz necklace you thought was sapphires. The setting is fake, too, but it's still a nice piece."

"An excellent choice." Molly put the scepter away and zipped the bag. "They'll look lovely with her mustache."

"My thought exactly." Chase chuckled and caught her hand. "Let's go, Princess. Next stop, Glyco."

And from there? Molly wondered, but didn't ask.

25

IT WAS NEARLY three o'clock when they arrived in Paris, the sky a storm-washed, silver-streaked black above the runway of the small airport Chase knew on the outskirts of the city. The seedier outskirts. He'd told Molly he had a pilot's license as they'd driven through the rainy darkness, the old Citroën's squeaky wipers making her teeth grit.

"Why can't we fly first class out of Orly?" she'd asked.

"We can't risk it," he'd said, backhanding fog off the inside of the windshield. "Not with Shehabi breathing down our neck."

"Oh," Molly said in a small voice. "Just how small is this small plane you're talking about?"

"Don't tell me." Chase cast her a sour look. "Please don't tell me you're afraid of flying."

"I wouldn't say afraid, exactly," Molly hedged, though God knew she wanted to. "I'd say . . . not fond."

"Don't worry, Princess. I fly even better than I drive."

"I was afraid you'd say that."

A jumbo jet was one thing, a two-seater not a hell of a lot bigger than her white Rolls limo—taxied out on the runway, no questions asked and no flight plan filed after Chase plunked down God-knew-how-much money—was a whole other ball game. Molly climbed aboard with her knees knocking and her heart in her throat, closed her eyes and kept them shut all the way across the Channel.

Which was just as well, Chase thought, glancing at her clenched jaw profile as he skimmed the little Beechcraft perilously close to the moon-silvered black waves. This was a tricky run, one he'd made dozens of times, but never with a passenger, and never with the Phantom murmuring agitatedly in his head.

It grew louder and shriller the nearer they came to Scotland. It was excited as hell about something. He didn't want to think what, but his knuckles were white when he put down to refuel. His whole body was shaking with strain when he landed at a strip outside Edinburgh.

He'd known Angus, the tough old ex-con who ran the place, since he'd pulled his first solo overseas job ten years ago. Angus came to Glyco to shoot grouse with Tony and drink with Cosmo. He gaped at Chase like he'd just landed a flying saucer when the Beechcraft taxied up on the apron and he came out of his grungy little office to meet it.

"Good lord. How long've you been ill?"

"Lovely to see you, too, Angus." Chase scowled as he swung his stiff body out of the cockpit. "I'll remember this next time you and Cosmo close the pubs. I need a car."

"And a week's sleep, by the look of you." Angus nodded at the rain-spattered windscreen of the Beechcraft. "Who's the lass with her head between her knees?"

"The Princess Royal of St. Cristobel."

"And I'm Bonny Prince Charlie." Angus chuckled and slapped him on the arm. "You'll be headed for Glyco?"

"Just as fast as you can get me there."

"I've just the thing," he said with a wink.

Angus had the Ferrari Chase had wished for in San Blanco, a gleaming, freshly waxed fire-engine red. A cold chill shot up his spine and stuck to the back of his neck when Angus drove it out of the hangar.

"If it's stolen, don't tell me," Molly said, clinging to his arm as he eased her on rubbery legs out of the Beechcraft and into the black leather bucket seat.

Chase didn't, just dropped a kiss on the top of her head and fastened her safety harness. By the time he'd shoved their bags in the back and swung in behind the wheel, she'd put her seat back and flung one arm over her eyes. She'd thrown up when they'd stopped to refuel, and what he could see of her face still looked pretty green. His plaid lay wadded and worried in her lap. Chase shook it out, spread it over her and pointed the Ferrari toward the Great North Road.

Molly was sound asleep before they left Edinburgh, snoring softly beside him through parted lips. Chase thought he could get used to the sound and smiled as he put on his sunglasses. One earpiece was gone and one lens was cracked. They'd been through hell—so had he and the princess—but they were still holding up.

The Phantom was singing, the shrill sound in his head setting his teeth on edge. The call grew louder and more excited with every mile he put behind them. When he stopped to buy gas and coffee it screamed. His ears were ringing by the time he slid in behind the wheel again.

Molly was still asleep, but stirring fitfully. He saved her a cup of coffee but gulped two as he drove. The caffeine took off some of the edge. He still had a few of Monsieur Bouvard's cigarettes, but his throat felt dry and tight enough. He had a bad feeling about taking the stone to Glyco, but it shrieked like a banshee when he considered turning around and heading back to Edinburgh.

The smell of coffee finally woke Molly. Her face was stuck to the seat, her stomach making ominous noises. It took her a minute to realize it was hunger, not nausea, and blink her eyes open.

When she did, she caught her breath. First at the dazzling play of light and shadow on the green hills flashing past the Ferrari, then at the sight of Chase when she turned her head and looked at him. His face was grim and gray, his jaw clenched. The silver highlights she'd thought were fire glow were still in his hair, most prominently at his temples.

He took one hand off the wheel and raked his hair back over his ears, unaware that she was watching him, until she said, "Hi."

He started and glanced at her, his eyes overbright, as if he was running a fever, but he smiled at her. "Feel better?"

"Fine. How about you?"

"Like I'm gonna crawl outta my skin." He swept a hand through his hair again. "We're almost home, Princess."

Maybe he was, but she wasn't. The realization made Molly's throat ache and her jaw clench. If he had a plan for what they'd do when they reached Glyco he hadn't told her, but it didn't matter. She had a plan of her own and it was very simple. He wasn't leaving her. She wasn't going to let him. Period. Not now, not ever.

If that didn't work, she wouldn't leave him. If necessary, she'd abdicate her throne. Either way, he wasn't getting rid of her. If Molly had learned nothing else being a princess, she'd learned how to be very persuasive. And very, *very* stubborn.

"Want me to drive for while?" she asked.

"No, thanks. It helps to have something else to think about. Here. Bought you something."

He picked up a white paper sack from the floor between his knees and passed it to her. His hand was shaking. Molly noticed it but didn't say anything.

There was a cup of coffee steaming inside and a blueberry Danish like the one she'd drowned in the Land Rover. Only yesterday. Only a lifetime ago.

"I love blueberry Danish." Molly took it out of the sack and bit the wrapper open, keeping her voice light as she popped the lid off the plastic cup. "You're a man after my own heart, Sanquist."

"I thought I already had it," he said, sliding her an edgy, sideways smile.

"I didn't think you wanted it."

"Oh, Princess," he said, a wistful sigh in his voice. "The things I want would scare the hell out of you."

The helicopter that suddenly came out of nowhere and swooped toward them head-on certainly scared the hell out of her. This time it was a red and white craft. Molly yelped, nearly jumped out of her seat belt and sloshed lukewarm coffee into her lap.

"Hang on." Chase downshifted and popped the clutch, squealing the tires in third gear.

The Ferrari shot forward like a rocket. *Oh, no. Oh, God. He was going to play chicken with the helicopter.* Molly gave up on her coffee and Danish, stuffed them in the bag, dumped it on the floor and grabbed the armrest on the door.

The chopper didn't waver. Neither did Chase. He clamped his hands on the wheel and punched the accelerator again, closing the gap between windshield and whipping rotor at almost sixty miles an hour. On a narrow, winding Highland road laughingly called a highway.

At the last possible second, a fraction before the scream in her throat came unstuck, the chopper lifted up and over the Ferrari, low enough and close enough to rock it on its springs. Molly whipped her head over her shoulder and saw it swoop around after them.

"Chicken!" Chase shouted. He worked the gears and the clutch again, squealing the transmission this time.

The Ferrari fishtailed through a right-hand curve, tires skidding on the verge above an icy blue burn tumbling through a rocky glen. The chopper overshot the curve and heeled sharply around behind them, its tail dipping and swinging dangerously close to the flank of the hill.

"Almost got you, you son of a bitch," Chase muttered into the rearview mirror, just as a dark figure leaned out of the right side of the chopper.

"Oh, Chase—" Molly gasped.

"I see him," he said, and slammed on the brakes.

The Ferrari did a one-eighty in the middle of the road, the chopper shooting past overhead, a burst of automatic gunfire ripping up the pavement where the Ferrari would have been. Molly's head spun and so did the tires, screeching and smoking as Chase straightened the nose and slingshoted the Ferrari through the next curve in the road.

How he'd done it, she couldn't imagine. She breathed a sigh of relief that they were still alive, felt a shiver of unease when she realized the chopper was falling behind.

"Why is it backing off?" Molly asked nervously.

"I don't know." Chase raked his fingers through his hair again, his gaze riveted on the mirror. "But all of a sudden I've got a bad feeling about all this."

So did Molly, a *very* bad feeling. "You don't suppose," she said slowly, "we've got somebody beside Shehabi and my uncle on our tail, do you?"

"Like who?"

"I don't know."

Chase took his hand off the wheel, twined his fingers through hers and laid her hand on his knee. She felt the tremble in his grip, and the odd, slipped-gear sensation again as the Ferrari rounded another curve. An open stretch of moor dotted with grazing sheep reared ahead of them. Rocky crags soared like a moonscape on the horizon, and a narrow finger of pewter-gray loch glimmered in the sun off to the left.

"If they're gonna come back," Chase said, flooring the accelerator, "they'll come back now."

He let go of Molly's hand and laid on the horn, scattering the sheep drifting across the road. Looking behind them between the seats Molly watched, but there was only the dust kicked up by the Ferarri's tires, and the slipped-gear feeling still gnawing at her. Until she turned around in her seat and the castle came into view; then she caught her breath.

"Is that Glyco?"

"What's left of it. The outer wall used to be twenty feet high all the way around."

Now it looked like a badly gnawed wheel of cheese, completely gone for a goodly distance on either side of the gatehouse. The moat was little more than a faint depression, the drawbridge a short, paved stretch leading into what had once been a bailey and was now a stretch of lawn before the keep. Stone steps led up to massive wooden doors that reminded Molly of the dungeons in her palace and made her shiver.

Chase laid on the horn again as the Ferrari shot across the drawbridge, past the graveled car park and onto the lawn.

When the doors of the keep swung inward and open, Natalie Savard was the first one through them. She wore a black turtleneck and slacks. Diello came behind her in jeans, a shirt and red sweater vest, then Inspector Francis in his usual gray suit and Cosmo in a brown tweed coat and trousers, his white hair almost silver in the sun. Last and bewildered-looking as always came Tony, as dark as Chase was fair, his glasses stuck on top of his head, his hands in the pockets of his corduroy pants.

"Mother!" Molly unhooked her seat belt, flung open her door as Chase skidded the Ferrari around in a sideways stop, leapt out of it and into Natalie's arms.

They were both crying and Diello was grumbling. Inspector Francis was talking into a walkie-talkie. The Phantom was trilling like the Vienna Boys Choir in Chase's head. It was a glorious sound. The stone was home, and it was happy.

So was Chase. So goddamn happy he was shaking. He wrapped his hands around the steering wheel, closed his eyes and leaned his forehead against it. He'd done it. He'd actually done it. Saved the Princess and brought the Phantom home to Glyco. Now all he had to do was figure out what the hell he was going to do with the stone. He'd already decided about Molly. Sort of.

"You did it, my boy," Cosmo said. "Damned if you didn't. Gave us all a turn, by God, but—"

His uncle broke off when Chase raised his head and looked at him.

"What *is* it? What's wrong?" Chase asked.

Cosmo reached into the car, grasped the rearview mirror and twisted it toward Chase. "Have a look."

Chase did, and felt his heart seize. His hair was laced with silver, particularly and heaviest at the temples. He'd gone gray overnight.

26

CHASE KNEW HOW and he knew why—the Phantom. Everything Jean-Marc had told him flashed through his head and turned his blood to ice.

"I'll get your bags," Cosmo said, reaching into the back.

"No." Chase snaked his hand between the seats and gripped his wrist. "Don't touch it. Don't even look at it."

Cosmo blinked at him. "The Phantom did this?"

"It wasn't the princess," Chase said, tugging the bags between the seats, "though God knows she tried."

Chase saw her walking up the steps behind Tony, between her mother and Diello, an arm around each of them.

"Nicely done, Chase," Inspector Francis said. "You gave my lads in St. Cristobel one devil of a time."

"Sorry about the mix-up in San Blanco, Inspector." Chase shouldered the backpack and Molly's black nylon bag.

"Quite all right," he said, falling into step with Chase as he started toward the house. "All's well that end's well."

"Never believe Scotland Yard," Cosmo whispered, slinging an arm around his shoulders. "Come along and have tea."

Just like this was a normal day, Chase thought ruefully. It wasn't the end, no matter what Francis said. There were too many threads left hanging—Shehabi and Karroll Savard, Tremayne and the red and white chopper. He intended to ask the inspector about them just as soon as he had a glass of water and asked Molly to marry him.

He was pretty sure Natalie would be pleased, and hoped to God she could keep Diello from killing him. He had no idea how they'd work out his past and Molly's future, but they'd find a way. If they couldn't, he'd steal her off the goddamn throne of St. Cristobel. He'd done it once.

The thought made him smile and his pulse quicken as he carried the Phantom over the threshold and it wept with joy. He had no idea why the jewel considered Scotland home. It was singing again, songs Chase knew by the melodies were old Highland ballads. Lovely, but he didn't want to hear them now.

He crossed the great hall and turned right toward the library with Cosmo and Francis, wondering if he could talk to the stone, convince it to shut up long enough for him to ask Molly to marry him. How about it, he asked the Phantom, but it was suddenly silent.

So was the library. The familiar warning chill laced up the back of Chase's neck as he stepped through the doorway. Too late, he saw the flash of a raised arm and a chrome pistol as he was blindsided from the left. The blow landed on his shoulder, driving him to his knees. Pain flashed down his arm, in his ears and in his head as both Molly and the Phantom screamed.

"There," Alec Tremayne said. "Now we're even."

Chase shook his head to clear it and blinked up at Tremayne. The bruise on Tremayne's forehead was the size of a lemon. He tucked his gun in his pants and stepped back, smiling, giving Chase a good look at Shehabi.

There were odd flashes of light where none should be on the dark wood paneling the walls between the built-in bookshelves, and a shadow that shouldn't be around the sheikh. He sat serenely in Cosmo's red leather chair with his knees crossed and his hands folded in his lap. The burnoose and silk robe he wore over a blue sweater and trousers were as white as Cosmo's hair.

Achmed held Tony and Diello against the fireplace with his scimitar. Habib, his left arm in a cast, loomed over Molly and Natalie on the window seat.

"Hail, hail, the gang's all here, except for Savard," Chase said shakily, as Cosmo gripped his elbow and helped him to his feet. "Where is he?"

"Someone," Shehabi replied with a smile, "has to run St. Cristobel for me."

Oh, Molly, oh, sweet, Chase prayed, oh, please don't say anything. But of course she did. It was one of the reasons he loved her.

"He won't be running it for long. And neither, Your Highness, will you."

"Silence, Princess," Shehabi replied coldly. "Or I will have Habib cut out your tongue."

On cue, Habib glowered. Molly glared at him, but kept quiet.

Chase glanced quickly around the library for something, anything, that would give him a clue how to get them out of here. His gaze caught on the red and white chopper on the lawn outside the open French doors, the rotor doing a slow downspin, the loch gleaming silver behind it at the bottom of the back garden.

That's why they'd backed off—they'd come the long way over the loch. Just as soon as John Francis had given them the all clear on the walkie-talkie. Too late, Chase realized he'd been Shehabi's man in the palace all along, that he'd known exactly where to find him and the Phantom, since Chase had stupidly—and trustingly—shown him the parchment.

"M-5, my ass," Chase said to him furiously. "You've been hiding under Shehabi's robe the whole time."

"Honest men are poor men," Francis replied with a shrug. "I finally got smart."

"Told you," Cosmo put in bitterly. "Never trust Scotland Yard."

Molly felt like a fool for having done exactly that. She felt the gears slide into place and her heart plummet to her toes as Inspector Francis pulled a gun out of his coat and waved Chase and his uncle into the room. Her mother caught her hand on the window seat and squeezed her fingers.

"If it's jewels you want," Molly said to him, "I can give you a collection to rival the Queen of England's."

"Thank you, Your Highness, but I'm interested in only one piece." Francis bobbed her a curt bow and took a step closer to Chase. "I'll take the brooch now and be on my way."

"Oh, you're good," Chase said to Shehabi. "You should write a book, Your Highness, like Donald Trump. I have the perfect title for you. *The Art of the Double Cross.*"

"I'm sure I don't know what you mean, Mr. Sanquist," he said languidly.

"And you, Inspector, of all people should know there's no honor among thieves." Chase tsked at him, his mind searching for a way out of this. "Shehabi has no intention of giving you the brooch. He plans to reunite it with the Phantom, to make them one and rule the world through the all-seeing, all-knowing Eye of Allah."

The stone didn't like that. It grumbled in Chase's head. Shehabi shot to his feet.

"Blasphemer!" he shouted. "You have no right to the sacred knowledge of my homeland!"

"You should've explained that to Achmed," Chase told him.

The big man went pale as Shehabi rounded on him, his robe swirling around him. Achmed dropped to his knees and crawled to kiss the sheikh's hem, babbling in Arabic. Shehabi drew a pistol from his robe and shot him.

"You." The sheikh waved the gun at Tremayne. "Over here and keep an eye on these two."

Chase saw the sod-you flicker in Alec's expression, but Alec kept his mouth shut, pulled his piece and took Achmed's post at the fireplace. Which suited Chase just fine. And Diello, too, if he read the gleam in his eyes right.

No one, as usual, was paying any attention to Tony. No one noticed him standing with his hands clasped behind him, his fingers closing around the handle of a poker. Not even the inspector, who had the same angle of advantage as Chase. The cool half smile on Francis's face raised another warning chill on the back of Chase's neck.

"Enough of this." Shehabi swung the gun on Chase, the scirocco swirling in his dark eyes. "Bring me the brooch and the Eye of Allah."

"They're in the bag," Chase said, reaching for the strap on his shoulder.

"Put it on the floor, open it and step back. I'll get them myself."

Chase moved into the center of the room, swinging the bag off his shoulder and dropping to one knee. The pool of blood beneath Achmed was spreading into the Aubusson carpet, mingling with the rusty stain left from poor old Ian Sanquist's suicide in 1760.

Was this the pendulum swinging back to make a correction, or a whole new arc? Chase wished the Phantom would clue him in, wished he dared look at Molly. He could just see her and a flash of sunlight from the window behind her gleaming on his plaid still thrown around her shoulders.

Chase unzipped the bag and pulled the top open. The brooch and the Phantom lay half-wrapped in a damp white towel atop Molly's ruined black sweater. The stone looked strangely dull and dark, its voice eerily silent.

"All yours, Your Highness," Chase said, pushing to his feet and stepping between Cosmo and Francis.

An ecstatic smile spread over Shehabi's bearded face. He tucked the gun inside his robe, knelt, touching his forehead to the floor and began to pray.

"Don't even think about it, Chase," Francis muttered in his ear. "I took the precaution of alerting the Yard as well as M-5. They should be along momentarily. You have as much chance of getting out of here as Shehabi."

"What about you and the brooch?"

"No one will suspect me. It will simply disappear from the evidence room."

"Not if Shehabi talks."

"He won't get the chance. Neither will you—or the princess—if you try anything."

"Touch her and I'll kill you."

"With what? Your bare hands?"

He could do it with less, Chase wanted to tell him, but didn't, for Shehabi raised himself up, dipped his hands into the bag and lifted the Phantom on his spread palms. A beam of sunlight vivid as a laser lanced through the window behind Molly's shoulder and struck the stone.

A dazzling bolt of white light leapt from it, and it burst into blinding blue flames. Shehabi screamed, dropped the stone and lurched to his feet, his beard and the sleeves of his robe on fire.

"My prince!" Habib cried, leaping toward him.

Francis was half a step behind him, and Chase a heartbeat ahead of him, smashing his elbow into the inspector's face. Blood spurted and Francis fell to his knees, clutching his broken nose. Cosmo grabbed the inspector's gun and whirled on Alec, just as Tony brought the poker down on

Alec's head. Habib joined Tremayne on the floor when Natalie stuck out her foot and tripped him and Molly whacked him over the head with an unabridged dictionary that sent up a puff of dust. Diello grabbed the edge of the carpet, yanked it off the floor and threw it over Shehabi, who was melting like a candle.

The black nylon bag had fallen over and spilled some of its contents on the parquet floor beneath the carpet. The Phantom was still throbbing, the brooch flickering beside it like a neon sign on the rumpled white towel.

Chase made a dive for the stone, and so did Molly. His hand closed over it first, then hers. Flashes of blue-white light pulsed between their fingers.

"My God." Molly snatched her hand back. "It's *pulsing.*"

"It does that when I get pissed. The same thing happened when the snow ledge came down on you. It does exactly what the sultan's curse said—gives me my heart's desire."

"Then how do you explain Shehabi?" Molly nodded over her shoulder at Diello and Tony rolling the moaning, shivering sheikh in the carpet. "You weren't anywhere near the Phantom. And you certainly didn't wish that on him."

"Hell, maybe I did, subconsciously or something. I don't know." Chase dragged both hands through his hair. He could almost feel himself turning grayer.

In the marbled mirror over the fireplace, he saw Francis holding a bloody handkerchief to his face and Cosmo standing over him with the gun. When the first faint wail of a siren drifted through the French doors, Molly clutched Chase's wrist, her eyes wide with panic.

"It's Scotland Yard and M-5. The inspector was covering his ass and double-crossing Shehabi." Chase scooped up the brooch and the Phantom, which was murmuring quietly now. He zipped them into the bag, then grabbed Molly's hand. "C'mon, Princess."

She ran with him halfway to the helicopter before she dug in her heels and pulled him around to face her. Chase felt his heart wrench at the tears in her eyes, the quaver in her chin, and knew what she was going to say.

"I can't go with you. I want to, but I can't leave my mother and Danny and your family to mop up this mess. And I can't leave my uncle on the throne."

"I was afraid you'd say that," Chase told her gently. "But the Phantom can't stay here—it can't stay *anywhere*—not after what it did to Shehabi."

"And what it's done to you." Molly brushed shaky fingertips through the hair at his temples. "I know that. You have to take it somewhere and get rid of it."

Chase didn't think that was possible, but he couldn't tell her that. He could only pull her into his arms, kiss her and tell her, "I love you."

"I love you." She clung to him, crying, her arms around his neck. "Come back to me."

"I will," Chase told her, though he wasn't at all sure he could.

He didn't know where he was going or how he was going to break free of the Phantom. He only knew he'd never be free of Molly. He kissed her, memorizing the shape and softness of her mouth, leapt into the red and white chopper and fired up the engine. It sputtered and caught, the rotor whirling and tossing the trees edging the garden.

Through the windscreen, Chase saw Molly back away, scraping her whipping hair out of her eyes with her hands. In the distance behind her, racing up the moor in a cloud of dust flickering with blue lights, came Scotland Yard and M-5. The Phantom shrieked on the seat beside him, pulsing dully but furiously inside the black nylon bag.

"You should have thought of this *before* you fried Shehabi," he told the stone, checking the gages and fastening his safety harness.

The Phantom stopped screaming and began wailing brokenheartedly. Chase wanted to weep with it, but swallowed the lump of tears aching in his throat and eased back on the stick and the collective.

The chopper rose off the ground, lifted past the trees and heeled around toward the loch. Chase was the pilot, but the Phantom was the navigator, murmuring, "East, east," in his head as the chopper skimmed away over the loch, its hull flashing in the sunlight.

27

IT TOOK MOLLY three months to realize Chase was never coming back. Ninety days without so much as a postcard for it to dawn on her that she'd been seduced, sweet-talked and swindled. Which proved beyond a shadow of a doubt that she was a fool, an absolute fool, and that no one ever died of a broken heart.

She wanted to, but she was too busy. There was her delayed coronation to tend to, followed by her uncle's trial. Much as she wanted to fling Karroll Savard into the dungeon and throw away the key, the cabinet and parliament wouldn't let her. She had to content herself with stripping him of his rank and all his titles and exiling him. Pretty tough stuff, but only a fraction of what he deserved.

Then there was the reconstruction of the south wing of the palace to oversee, and St. Cristobel's financial crisis to solve. Molly signed over all her personal assets to the national treasury, which helped in the short term. Long-term loans were arranged with the World Bank. She steered clear of foreign aid, generously offered by all and sundry. She'd learned the hard way what disaster foreign influence could wreck.

Only because it was a matter of state did she send gifts, flowers and a representative to Shehabi's funeral. She delegated the sympathy letters to his heirs and seventeen wives to one of her secretaries. She was allowed to depose for John Francis and Alec Tremayne's trials. They were sentenced to the same prison. Poetic justice, Molly thought.

She lost interest in skating, food, pretty much everything but work. Falling brain-dead into bed every night kept her from dreaming about Chase. Her only comfort was figuring that by now the Phantom had probably turned him white-headed.

In July, his cousin Tony and his uncle Cosmo paid a state visit to St. Cristobel, something Molly couldn't avoid since they were distantly related. Tony was charming and considerate and handsome as the devil, as dark as Chase was fair.

"We haven't heard a word from him," he told Molly. "I'll let you know the minute we do."

"Don't bother. I couldn't care less," she told him, and almost meant it.

The Earl of Glyco's two-week visit left the aristocratic ladies of St. Cristobel panting. Cosmo was a rake and a rapscallion and Molly adored him, even though he dropped Chase's name every five minutes. She even let him pinch her and tell her she had bottom. He took her to visit Jean-Marc DuValle, who turned out to be her father's secret, special friend and Otto's grandfather.

Molly wasn't surprised, and she was relieved—oh, so relieved—when Cosmo showed her Crown Prince Sandor I's proclamation. She told him the Sanquists were welcome to the Phantom, that if Chase ever deigned to show his face at Glyco and stop worrying his family she wouldn't fight them for it. She never wanted to see it again. Ever. And meant it.

By the end of August, when the first snows began to fall in the mountains, she could pass whole days and only think about Chase once or twice. By October, when Natalie came from Chicago with an invitation from Cosmo to come shoot grouse at Glyco, Molly surprised her by happily agreeing.

"Why shouldn't I go?" she asked, glancing up at her thunderstruck mother from the latest financial forecasts.

They were bleak, but not as dismal as they'd been six months ago. "It's not like Chase is going to be there. I like Tony and I love Cosmo and I could use a break."

"Never mind, then." Natalie took a folded sheet of paper out of her purse and tore it in half. "I don't need this."

"What is it?"

"The list I made of all the reasons you should go."

Tony was waiting for them at Glyco with Cosmo. He was brown as a nut, just back from a dig near the Libyan border. The Egyptian government had made a tremendous find, a cache of tombs in the middle of an oil field they'd wrestled away from a wacko American billionare. The catacombs beneath an acropolis on an escarpment predated the first Egyptian dynasty by several thousand years.

Molly smiled and listened and nodded off to sleep in Cosmo's red leather chair. She slept most of the next day, too, ate like a plow horse and spent the morning of her second full day at Glyco fishing the loch with Cosmo. Her mother and Danny had gone shooting with Tony. Molly never wanted to see another gun so long as she lived.

The only thing she caught was a sunburn, and a pinch on the fanny when she got out of the boat. She slapped Cosmo's hand. He laughed and jostled her against him.

"You're a grand lass. Nothing like a woman with bottom."

That's what fell out of her, when Cosmo swept her into the library and she saw Chase standing in front of the fireplace gazing into the flames, one foot on the hearth, the other on the mantel. The bottom of her heart and her carefully reconstructed life.

"Oh, good. You've arrived," Cosmo said cheerfully, pushing Molly into the room. "Don't carve him up too bad, lass. He's my only source of income."

He shut the doors behind her. And locked them. Chase lifted his head and smiled at her, the silver in his hair glinting in the sunlight streaming past the window seat.

"Hello, Princess. I see you're still wearing my plaid."

She almost said her name was Molly, but decided princess suited her just fine. The pang she felt looking at him didn't. He'd lost twenty pounds at least, and his hair—oh, his hair.

"It's warm." Molly clutched the ends of the plaid draped around her neck defensively. "And Scotland is damn cold."

Getting colder by the minute, Chase thought, feeling his heart start to pound as he watched her eyes change from seafoam green to icy, angry amber. He didn't blame her. Not one bit. Her cheeks were flushed. He hoped with cold.

"I brought back your diamond."

"It's not mine," she shot back. "It never was. Cosmo showed me the proclamation. I've submitted a copy to the parliament for their review. St. Cristobel won't contest ownership. The Phantom is yours and you're damn welcome to it. I never want to see it again."

Her chin was quavering and so was her voice. With fury, and something else it took Chase a minute to recognize was jealousy. His heart flipped, but he stayed where he was, gripping the mantel to keep from leaping across the room to embrace her and press his mouth to the pulse he could see drumming in the hollow of her throat.

"Then I'll trade you even up. My plaid for the Phantom."

"I don't want your damn plaid!" Molly whipped it off her neck and threw it at him. He caught it in one hand and hung it around his neck. "I want you. It means my mother raised a fool, but I—"

Chase crossed the room and swept her into his arms before Molly even saw him move. She threw her arms around him and buried her face in his chest, gasping to keep from crying and inhaling—sandalwood, she thought it was.

"You said you'd come back, but you didn't. Why didn't you write to me? Or call me? Or—"

"I couldn't." Chase lifted his head from hers and pressed a finger to her lips. "There aren't many phones in Tibet, and the mail moves by yak."

"Oh, *sure* you went to Tibet. To a monastery, I suppose."

"Yes, as a matter of fact. The Phantom took me there. The monks know the stone well."

She cocked one eyebrow dubiously. "The *Phantom* took you to Tibet?"

"That's not its name, but it's agreed to answer to it."

"Why," Molly asked, turning her chin warily to one side, "am I hearing the *Twilight Zone* theme in my head?"

"Do you really want to talk about this now?" Chase bent his head toward her, his sapphire eyes smoky and half-lidded. "I've been waiting six months to finish."

"Finish what?" Molly asked puzzledly, then caught her breath, and said with a long sigh, "Oh. *Finish.*"

"Unlock the door, Cosmo," Chase called, swooping her up in his arms.

Molly yelped, laughing with joy, and looped an arm around his shoulders. Cosmo pushed the library doors inward, a merry conspirator's grin on his face.

"Be gentle with him, lass," he called behind them, as Chase carried her through the great hall and up the stairs. "He's a bit weak yet."

Not that Molly could tell. He was hardly winded when he dumped her on the bed in her guest room and went to lock the door. When it clicked and he turned toward her, peeling off his thick, beige sweater, her heart started to race.

"After the hell you put me through," she teased, drawing her legs up and tucking them beneath her, "I should make you wait another six months."

"No can do, Princess." He unsnapped and unzipped his jeans, the metallic rip sending a shiver up Molly's back. "My phenomenal self-control ain't what it used to be."

"Prove it," she murmured, reaching for the buttons on her green and yellow flannel shirt.

Chase dropped to his knees beside the bed and finished undoing them, pressing his lips to the pulse fluttering in her throat. She slipped her fingers into his hair and cupped his mouth to her breasts. He nuzzled her softly, throbbing with need and aching with love. When she sighed onto her back and drew him with her, he laughed and rolled with her onto the bed, groping at her clothes, growling in her ear, making her laugh with him.

By the time he wrestled them both out of their clothes, Molly's eyes were shining, her hair a glorious mess of tousled, gold-streaked brown. Her breasts were flushed and her nipples peaked against his chest.

"Oh Molly, oh sweet." Chase buried his face in the curve of her neck and shivered. "I can't wait. I'm sorry, but I can't."

"You don't have to." She wrapped her arms around his neck, opening her mouth for him as she opened her legs.

Chase drove his body into hers, his tongue beneath hers. Molly took his weight, his frantic thrusts, and his ragged breath with a smug, Serene Highness smile, and happy tears jeweling on her lashes when he raised his head from the curve of her neck.

"There goes my proclamation for outstanding service." Chase smiled as she laughed, feeling her muscles tightening around him. "Guess I'll have to earn another one."

"Sorry. Only one to a customer. I have something else in mind for you."

"Do I get conjugal visits in the dungeon?"

She laughed again. Chase felt himself tighten, threaded his fingers through her hair and spread it on the pillow. The sunlight streaming through the window turned the strands to molten gold in his hands.

"I have this vacant grand duchy I'm trying to unload." Molly wagged her eyebrows and twined her arms around his neck. "Interested?"

"I thought you made me a count."

"You can be both."

"Why would I want to be?"

"I can't marry a count, but I can marry a grand duke."

"How about a thief?"

"Only if he's a grand duke."

"Does it pay anything? I'm the sole support of my feeble old white-headed uncle, y'know."

"There's no salary. Just fringe benefits." She smiled, her eyes glowing. "Like unlimited conjugal visits."

"Tempting," Chase murmured, nibbling her bottom lip. "I'll think about it."

Before she could squawk, he slipped his hands under her and rolled on his back, taking her with him and sliding deeper inside her, hard again and hot. Her breath caught and her eyes widened with surprise and pleasure. She sighed and smiled and spread her hands on his chest, her nipples peaked and ready to be kissed.

"Amuse yourself," Chase murmured, pushing himself up on his hands to nuzzle her left breast. "While I consider your offer."

There was no question that he'd take it, or that he loved her. He told her so, over and over, kissing the words into her throat and her breasts while he cupped her hips and rocked her back and forth, filling her, loving her and healing her heart.

He told her twice more before he let her rest, rolling her into his arms, warm and sticky and blissfully exhausted. Molly fell asleep listening to his heartbeat, but woke up alone. Long beams of dusty, late afternoon sun slanted across the foot of the bed, jeweling on the heather tones of his plaid crumpled up with the twisted bedclothes.

She smiled and stretched, knowing he'd be back. When he returned, belted into a paisley dressing gown, he had a silver tray in his hands. He locked the door again and turned toward her, grinning and dipping the tray toward her so she could see what was on it—a white plastic cup and a blueberry Danish in a cheap cellophane wrapper.

"Oh, Chase." Molly laughed delightedly, punched up the pillows and leaned against them, tucking the covers around her breasts.

He put the tray on her lap and settled down beside her, pressing a kiss to her temple as his arm went around her shoulders. Molly opened the Danish, gave him the first bite, took one of her own and said, "Tell me about Tibet."

He did, briefly. He told her about the monks, the thin, rarefied air, how he'd learned to talk to and listen to the Phantom.

"It took a while for us to come to terms," he explained. "It's been around a very long time, y'know. Took it all these months to give me its life history."

"You mean I was right?" Molly swallowed hard around the last bite of Danish. "It's alive?"

"Sentient is a better word. It's very wise. It knows a lot of stuff. It's been abused, but it never meant to hurt anyone. Except Shehabi. It knew what he had in mind."

"So it's enchanted, right?" Molly asked, trying to understand. "I mean, it has to be, doesn't it?"

"Kinda sorta." Chase tipped one hand from side to side.

"I think I've heard enough for now." Molly put the tray aside, laid her head on Chase's shoulder and thought about everything he'd told her. "I think you should take it back to Tibet. It may be very wise, but it could be very dangerous if it falls into the wrong hands again."

"Good idea, if it'll go. It has a mind of its own, you know." Chase kissed the top of her head. "If the Phantom agrees, we'll take it back on our honeymoon."

"Excuse me." Molly held up one finger. "When did you ask me to marry you?"

"I accepted your offer. I didn't think I had to ask."

"You not only have to ask *me*, you have to ask the parliament of St. Cristobel. Actually you have to submit a formal request. In triplicate. You have to be interviewed and pass a medical and a psychological evaluation."

Chase arched an eyebrow at her. "Even if I'm a grand duke?"

"*Especially* if you're a grand duke."

"That could be tricky. I'll ace the physical but I'll probably flunk the psychological."

"Based on everything you've told me, I'd say that's a strong possibility."

Chase scratched his chin thoughtfully, then glanced at her sideways. "Wanna elope?"

"I thought you'd never ask."

"This is how we do it in the Highlands." He tugged his plaid off the foot of the bed and looped it around her shoulders. "I've captured you and you're mine. All I have to do is keep you prisoner in this bed until I make you pregnant, then the clan chief, the Laird of Glyco, will consider you my duly wedded wife."

"Let me guess." Molly laughed. "Cosmo is the chief."

"You got it." Chase grinned and kissed her. "And you got me, Princess."

"My name," she murmured, pulling him down in the bed beside her, "is Molly."

COMING NEXT MONTH

#513 HEARTSTRUCK Elise Title
The Hart Girls Book 2

Fired from her glitzy D.C. news anchor job and then dumped by
her "loving" fiancé, a downhearted Julie Hart slunk home to Pittsville.
The only job she could land was hosting "Pittsville Patter." Life was
the *pits*...until she met her gorgeous, blue-eyed, six-foot cohost,
Ben Sandler!

#514 A KISS IN THE DARK Tiffany White

For extra cash, Brittany Astor took an evening job reading aloud.
Only, her employer wasn't the sweet little old lady she'd imagined, but
notorious, sexy Ethan Moss—the man she'd been secretly lusting after
for years! He'd been temporarily blinded and needed someone to help
fill his time. For timid, plain Brittany, this was her chance to seduce
Ethan...but could she win him?

#515 LADY OF THE NIGHT Kate Hoffmann

Annabeth Dupree was *not* a call girl! Just because she'd inherited a
house of ill repute, didn't mean she'd reopened the business. So when
Zach Tanner threatened to have Annabeth arrested, she got mad. And
madder still when she realized she was falling for a man who thought
she was a fallen woman.

#516 THE BOUNTY HUNTER Vicki Lewis Thompson

Bounty hunter Gabe Escalante was hot on the trail of a dangerous criminal. When he suspected gorgeous Dallas Wade was the next target, he
vowed to watch over her. But soon Gabe wanted to be more than her
bodyguard. Not only her life was at stake now...so was his heart.

AVAILABLE NOW:

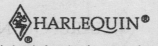
HARLEQUIN®

Don't miss these Harlequin favorites by some of our most distinguished authors!
And now you can receive a discount by ordering two or more titles!

HT#25483	BABYCAKES by Glenda Sanders	$2.99	☐
HT#25559	JUST ANOTHER PRETTY FACE by Candace Schuler	$2.99	☐
HP#11608	SUMMER STORMS by Emma Goldrick	$2.99	☐
HP#11632	THE SHINING OF LOVE by Emma Darcy	$2.99	☐
HR#03265	HERO ON THE LOOSE by Rebecca Winters	$2.89	☐
HR#03268	THE BAD PENNY by Susan Fox	$2.99	☐
HS#70532	TOUCH THE DAWN by Karen Young	$3.39	☐
HS#70576	ANGELS IN THE LIGHT by Margot Dalton	$3.50	☐
HI#22249	MUSIC OF THE MIST by Laura Pender	$2.99	☐
HI#22267	CUTTING EDGE by Caroline Burnes	$2.99	☐
HAR#16489	DADDY'S LITTLE DIVIDEND by Elda Minger	$3.50	☐
HAR#16525	CINDERMAN by Anne Stuart	$3.50	☐
HH#28801	PROVIDENCE by Miranda Jarrett	$3.99	☐
HH#28775	A WARRIOR'S QUEST by Margaret Moore	$3.99	☐
	(limited quantities available on certain titles)		

TOTAL AMOUNT	$
DEDUCT: 10% DISCOUNT FOR 2+ BOOKS	$
POSTAGE & HANDLING	$
($1.00 for one book, 50¢ for each additional)	
APPLICABLE TAXES*	$_____
TOTAL PAYABLE	$_____
(check or money order—please do not send cash)	

To order, complete this form and send it, along with a check or money order for the total above, payable to Harlequin Books, to: **In the U.S.:** 3010 Walden Avenue, P.O. Box 9047, Buffalo, NY 14269-9047; **In Canada:** P.O. Box 613, Fort Erie, Ontario, L2A 5X3.

Name: _____

Address: _____ City: _____

State/Prov.: _____ Zip/Postal Code: _____

*New York residents remit applicable sales taxes.
  Canadian residents remit applicable GST and provincial taxes.

HBACK-OD

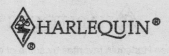

EDGE OF ETERNITY
Jasmine Cresswell

Two years after their divorce, David Powell
and Eve Graham met again in Eternity,
Massachusetts—and this time there was magic
between them. But David was tied up in a
murder that no amount of small-town gossip
could free him from. When Eve was pulled into
the frenzy, he knew he had to come up with
some answers—including how to convince her
they should marry again...this time for keeps.

EDGE OF ETERNITY, available in
November from Intrigue, is the sixth book in
Harlequin's exciting new cross-line series,
WEDDINGS, INC.

Be sure to look for the final book, **VOWS,** by
Margaret Moore (Harlequin Historical #248),
coming in December.

"HOORAY FOR HOLLYWOOD" SWEEPSTAKES

HERE'S HOW THE SWEEPSTAKES WORKS

OFFICIAL RULES — NO PURCHASE NECESSARY

To enter, complete an Official Entry Form or hand print on a 3" x 5" card the words "HOORAY FOR HOLLYWOOD", your name and address and mail your entry in the pre-addressed envelope (if provided) or to: "Hooray for Hollywood" Sweepstakes, P.O. Box 9076, Buffalo, NY 14269-9076 or "Hooray for Hollywood" Sweepstakes, P.O. Box 637, Fort Erie, Ontario L2A 5X3. Entries must be sent via First Class Mail and be received no later than 12/31/94. No liability is assumed for lost, late or misdirected mail.

Winners will be selected in random drawings to be conducted no later than January 31, 1995 from all eligible entries received.

Grand Prize: A 7-day/6-night trip for 2 to Los Angeles, CA including round trip air transportation from commercial airport nearest winner's residence, accommodations at the Regent Beverly Wilshire Hotel, free rental car, and $1,000 spending money. (Approximate prize value which will vary dependent upon winner's residence: $5,400.00 U.S.); 500 Second Prizes: A pair of "Hollywood Star" sunglasses (prize value: $9.95 U.S. each). Winner selection is under the supervision of D.L. Blair, Inc., an independent judging organization, whose decisions are final. Grand Prize travelers must sign and return a release of liability prior to traveling. Trip must be taken by 2/1/96 and is subject to airline schedules and accommodations availability.

Sweepstakes offer is open to residents of the U.S. (except Puerto Rico) and Canada who are 18 years of age or older, except employees and immediate family members of Harlequin Enterprises, Ltd., its affiliates, subsidiaries, and all agencies, entities or persons connected with the use, marketing or conduct of this sweepstakes. All federal, state, provincial, municipal and local laws apply. Offer void wherever prohibited by law. Taxes and/or duties are the sole responsibility of the winners. Any litigation within the province of Quebec respecting the conduct and awarding of prizes may be submitted to the Regie des loteries et courses du Quebec. All prizes will be awarded; winners will be notified by mail. No substitution of prizes are permitted. Odds of winning are dependent upon the number of eligible entries received.

Potential grand prize winner must sign and return an Affidavit of Eligibility within 30 days of notification. In the event of non-compliance within this time period, prize may be awarded to an alternate winner. Prize notification returned as undeliverable may result in the awarding of prize to an alternate winner. By acceptance of their prize, winners consent to use of their names, photographs, or likenesses for purpose of advertising, trade and promotion on behalf of Harlequin Enterprises, Ltd., without further compensation unless prohibited by law. A Canadian winner must correctly answer an arithmetical skill-testing question in order to be awarded the prize.

For a list of winners (available after 2/28/95), send a separate stamped, self-addressed envelope to: Hooray for Hollywood Sweepstakes 3252 Winners, P.O. Box 4200, Blair, NE 68009.

CBSRLS

OFFICIAL ENTRY COUPON

"Hooray for Hollywood"
SWEEPSTAKES!

Yes, I'd love to win the Grand Prize — a vacation in Hollywood —
or one of 500 pairs of "sunglasses of the stars"! Please enter me
in the sweepstakes!

This entry must be received by December 31, 1994.
Winners will be notified by January 31, 1995.

Name _____

Address _____ Apt. _____

City _____

State/Prov. _____ Zip/Postal Code _____

Daytime phone number _____
(area code)

Account # _____

Return entries with invoice in envelope provided. Each book
in this shipment has two entry coupons — and the more
coupons you enter, the better your chances of winning!

DIRCBS